Children of the Wrong Time

Flavia Idà

Cover design © 2017 by Niki Lenhart
nikilen-designs.com

Published by Paper Angel Press
paperangelpress.com

ISBN 978-1-944412-66-1 (Trade Paperback)

10 9 8 7 6 5 4 3 2

FIRST EDITION

For more information about the author and her work visit:
flaviasvoice.com

Dedication

For my grandson Alexander

With thanks to Steven Radecki for his helpful suggestions and unflagging patience.
With thanks to Dan Langton for his keen-eyed advice.
With thanks to Niki Lenhart for her beautiful artwork.

ONE

MICHAEL HOLMES AND NORA SAVINS passed through the bottleneck of the security checkpoint, stepped into the ornate atrium of the Department of Vital Privileges, and looked at the white marble statue of the Founding Father.

The Founding Father beamed down on them above the busy crowd, a handsome young man with long black hair, who carried in one hand an ancient movie script rolled up into a scroll and, in the other hand, an auto racer's helmet. The wreath of laurels at his feet hadn't wilted since the national celebration of his birthday.

"Keanu Reeves," Michael said reverently. "Best thing America ever gave us."

He pointed at the inscription carved in tall letters on the base of the life-sized statue. "And his words that began it all."

He recited the movie line, known to every citizen older than six.

"You need a license to drive, you need a license to fish, you need a license to own a dog, but any moron can become a parent."

Under the inscription he read the First Law of the Republic: *"Never Again Any Moron."*

Behind the statue was the Republic's flag, a field of blue showing an ancestry chart with golden stars in place of family names.

Michael looked at Nora. "Are you all right?"

Nora made a small headshake for *no*.

"Do I look okay?" she asked.

"I told you, you look great."

"Yeah, well, all you have to do is pick the blue suit over the grey suit. Me, I have to be conservative, but not dowdy; feminine, but not trampy …"

Michael brushed aside her concerns with a good-natured laugh.

"Come on, Grumps. Smile."

He glanced at his holofolder marked *Reproduction – Application One.*

"Here we go," he said softly. He passed his hand over the elevator plaque and stepped in after her.

Anxiety had dropped a wall between them. Too many worries, too many hopes, made noise in their minds. Was he a good provider, and did they really say he must provide for eighteen years? Was she a good homemaker, and did they really say she must make a home for eighteen years?

The elevator was full of people, each headed to their private petition. One elderly couple, the husband in a medchair, was certainly on their way to the Office of End-of-Life Privileges. The man was breathing with difficulty, a portable oxygen mask over his face. The woman wore a look of quiet anguish.

Nora eyed them on the sly. She thought it seemed cruel that a man that sick should be required to bring his application in person; but, of course, it was because anyone might make the application in his name with malice aforethought.

Would these two be granted their License for End-Of-Life Privileges? she wondered. Would she and Michael one day have to bring a similar application?

The elevator bell dinged; the doors swooshed open. People streamed down the hallway in a mingled chatter of voices. Michael and Nora found the door of the office marked *Reproduction – Application One*. Michael bent to kiss Nora's cheek, then leaned into the blinking Sesame panel and said, "Open".

From behind a cluttered desk, a brisk-looking woman motioned them to come in. Her hair was in an outdated French updo, and it seemed an oddly vain thing that she wore her electronic ID tag on what looked like a gold chain.

"Mr. Holmes, Miss Savins. I'm Linda Yamasaki. Please have a seat."

Michael let Nora sit first, in one of the two comfortable chairs on this side of the desk. Comfortable or not, Nora thought, all those who sat in those chairs felt anything but comfortable. She eyed the two piles of holofolders that framed Mrs. Yamasaki. How many of those folders were destined for the incinerator?

"Our current deferment rate is sixty-four percent," Mrs. Yamasaki said genially, as if reading her mind. "When the Parenthood Laws were first introduced, the rate was almost eighty percent."

Nora tried to smile. Michael nodded to Mrs. Yamasaki.

"Very encouraging," he said pleasantly.

Nora relaxed a bit. Unlike her, Michael was always at ease with others. It seemed that, by choosing him as the speaker, she had already made one good step toward the License. Thank God — no, wrong expression.

"So then. I see that you, Mr. Holmes, are thirty-one, you have an Advanced Degree in Economics, and a full-time job as Chief Product Manager at Lantym Software. You, Miss Savins, are twenty-six, you have a Specialized Degree in English, and you currently teach for the Curie School District, Rigoberta Menchu High. It's a part-time position, but since you are the applicant *mother*, that is perfectly fine."

She pointed at the holofolders on her left, lined up in a slotted bin marked "Eyes Only."

"The biometrics came in last week, and so did the background checks from the Provincial Bureau and from the Department of Internal Investigations. So far everything's where it should be. It's a good start."

She handed Michael a FyreTel tablet.

"Here are the contacts of your certified observers. Doctor Canetti is your general practitioner; she will refer you to the specialists. Doctor Patel is your general psychologist; he will direct you to the various branches. You should get in touch with Dr. Canetti and Dr. Patel at your earliest convenience, for your first medical exam and your intake therapy session. You also have the contacts of your Parenting Classes Consortium and of the Reproductive Bank. They will provide you with the list of certified surrogates, maternal and paternal. All the offices are within reasonable distance of each other, to minimize time and traffic."

"Whew," Michael said, "It's a full-time job."

"As it should be," Mrs. Yamasaki replied somewhat archly. "It's not too much to ask for your child, is it?"

"Oh, not at all," Michael agreed. "*The task of making a happy human —*"

"— *must start as soon as humanly possible,*" Nora quickly completed the Second Law of the Republic. "Believe me, nobody wants that more than Michael and me."

Michael and *I*, she thought frantically. Did an English teacher have to make a mistake like that right in front of this woman?

Mrs. Yamasaki was looking over the application. At last, with a bit of a flourish, she placed the holofolder in the slotted bin at her right side. Nora, the granddaughter of lapsed Irish Catholics, thought it seemed like a good omen: on Judgment Day, the souls of the saved went to Jesus' right side.

"All's in place, then," Michael said with some relief.

"All's in place, Mr. Holmes. Parenthood is the most important job on the planet," she recited for the tenth time that morning. "It's a fundamental human right, but one that has become — and not a moment too soon — a human right that must be *earned*. Being a parent takes time, takes money, takes patience, takes community, and takes commitment."

She turned toward a smaller desk behind her, where a profusion of family photos in antique twenty-first-century frames attested to her competence.

"As for the rewards, of course … My husband and I were granted the License four times, not an easy thing in this age of mandated restrictions."

For her next sentence, she looked directly at Nora.

"We had to apply twice for our first child. There's no shame attached to the number of times you apply."

Why did it sound sanctimonious instead of encouraging? Nora wondered.

"You have a busy year ahead of you," Mrs. Yamasaki concluded, again for the tenth time that morning. "If all goes well, it will be my pleasure to hand you your License a year from today."

"We can't wait to get started," Michael said, shaking her hand. "Thank you for your time, Mrs. Yamasaki."

Nora shook hands after him. "Thank you ... Thank you very much."

On their way out of the office, they crossed the next couple of applicants, no less anxious and no less hopeful.

Nora tried to gauge their chances. They seemed young enough to be still in college — the minimum required to apply for the License was a Level 2 Bachelor's degree — and there was a clear streak of anger in the way the young man pushed his partner aside to go in first. Two strikes, Nora thought; the young woman's rainbow eyeshadow could very well be the third.

Michael did a light skip on his way out of the elevator for sheer good feeling.

"So, what do we do now?" Nora asked. "Should we start going thru our contacts? The reproductive bank, the doctor, the psychologist?"

"No, let's celebrate. Let's have lunch someplace fancy. I hear they've opened a great ethnic restaurant on Jane Goodall Boulevard."

"What kind of ethnic?"

"American. It's called 'The Iowa State Fair'."

"I'm not really hungry," Nora said. She made a vague gesture at the building behind them. "To think that that woman up there has our future stashed away in her files ..."

Michael's face turned serious. He stopped in front of her, a head taller, and thirty pounds heavier than she was, as recommended by the Manual of Evolutionary Parameters.

"Nora, don't. She's not the one who decides. *We* decide to play by the rules; ergo, *we* make our future. It's always been like that."

"Only, the rules have somewhat changed. Whatever happened to having a child because you chose to have a child, when you chose, and with whomever you chose?"

"Those were the bad old days. All those children of unmarried teens, of drug addicts and alcoholics and abusers … None of that now. No more babies born to any moron with a gonad, no more street children. *If you cannot feed them, you are not allowed to breed them.*"

The Third Law of the Republic had been paraphrased from a maxim of one of the Founding Mothers, the American Judge Judy Sheindlin.

"Yes," Nora muttered. "I know my catechism."

"Don't use that word," Michael chided. "Don't get into that mindset. You know we are required not to give our child a religious education of any kind until he's eighteen … he or she, whatever comes."

"Whatever comes," Nora echoed. "As if our Mrs. Yamasaki is going to overlook the box marked 'Gender Preference'."

Michael looked up at the statue of the Founding Father and smiled conspiratorially.

"Forgive her, Keanu. She's letting her emotions get away with her … Women, can't be helped, so say the experts."

The sharp autumn light glinted on the buildings outside, and the sun was uncomfortably hot. There had been very little rain for two years in a row. The Department of Household Sustainability would most certainly shut down again half of the water supply to their house. Bicycles, mopeds, and pedicabs darted along the streets under orange and lemon trees ready to bud.

Nora shrunk against Michael's side and let all her worries slide into his solid frame.

"That's my girl," he praised.

He opened the door for her on the passenger side of their Lakota XL.

"The Iowa State Fair it is, then."

TWO

S EATED ON HAY BALES, while waiting for their order, Michael pulled out of his vest pocket the small blue box with the ring inside.

"Step One, Application. Step Two, Engagement. Step Three, Marriage."

He wanted to sound pedantic, a parody of Mrs. Yamasaki, but he was smiling like a little boy. He slipped the ring onto Nora's finger.

"Miss Savins, will you marry me?"

"Oh Michael, this is gorgeous," she sighed. "Yes, Mr. Holmes, I do believe I will marry you."

Nora had long expected that Step Two, as she expected the prenuptial agreement that went with the engagement. The agreement was not mandatory, but the great majority of couples drew one up without objections.

To think, she wondered, that women were once clueless enough to refuse the agreement on the grounds that it would "hex" their marriage, only to have to fight for every bit of property due to them if the marriage failed — and, back then, the rate of failure was almost sixty percent.

Michael had made an easy chore of their prenup. He was comfortably rooted in logic, and could be counted upon to do all that was needed in "the marathon", and at the time it was needed.

Parenthood, as the Republic meant it, offered obstacles of equal measure for all contenders — and an all-important prize: the Parenting License earned and cherished as a proud blessing.

We have done all that our country requires in order to raise her citizens in the best possible manner. We have worked hard to give our children the best possible start in a world of too many unknowns.

Nora moved her hand to make the ring shine. It was as beautiful as it was supposed to be, costing the appropriate number of months off the salary of the Chief Product Manager in one of the nation's most prestigious tech firms. Michael looked delighted and proud. She was comforted to find between them affection, the most important thing counted upon for a successful marriage.

"Generation Forth," the media praised, "has found security in the curtailing of those variables that so often turned against past generations. The dangerous delusion of 'love at first sight' now appeals only to teenagers, who, for that reason, are barred from the privilege of reproduction until they become adults. For that same reason, it's the parents themselves who have willingly become the enforcers of mandated contraception for their minor children. As the Fourth Law reminds us, '*Unchecked libido is unqualified disaster.*'"

Four years had passed since Michael and Nora had met through the hands-on services of a state-certified matchmaker. It was the minimum recommended waiting time from first encounter to engagement. The evolutionary psychologists had agreed that four years was as long as it took for the initial near-manic high of infatuation to subside. Once the "hormonal goggles" wore off, it was time to sift through what was left, and determine whether what was left appeared strong enough to sustain a marriage.

At first, the wait had seemed endless. Lovers are always in a hurry to say, "Forever." But the time could be filled by taking some of the initial steps of the marathon. Against her every expectation, Nora had enjoyed her cooking classes, while Michael had breezed through his courses in automotive repair.

Nora had seen Michael unkempt and constipated in the morning, and Michael had learned to ignore Nora's pantyhose on the towel rack. They had resolved arguments over what to have for dinner, and what to spend on the car. They had survived his layoff and her PMS. In the end, the "chemistry" had held, their friendship had taken root in spite of everything.

It hadn't been luck. It had been a systematic search for the most suitable mate, made with the same consideration as the search for the most suitable job or the most suitable mortgage lender. The motto of the Republic was "From Random Chance to Rational Choice."

Indeed, they had a busy year ahead of them; but it was going to seem like a small length of time until their License hung in the nursery.

A cheerful server dressed in faux-denim overalls came to bring their entrées, served on china plates: three corndogs each, elegantly spaced and surrounded by wisps of mustard.

"Four weeks from now?" Michael asked, nuzzling Nora's cheek.

Nora smiled. "Four weeks from now."

Michael took a bite of his corndog. "Hmmm, these are delicious … Last time I had corn was during my business trip to New York."

"And gender preference?" he asked then, without looking at her. It was the only point on which they were in disagreement: Nora wanted a girl; Michael wanted a boy.

Nora was in no mood to start the disagreement again, not today.

"We can always leave it to nature," she said. "Or flip a coin."

Michael shook his head. "No. You don't want *this* random chance hanging between us for the rest of our lives. It's much too important."

Nora stopped eating. "My parents too would love a girl for a firstborn … That's one more advantage, isn't it? Two more people who would be pleased?"

A flash of annoyance crossed Michael's handsome features.

"We've talked about all this already. We should let the *grandparents* pick the gender?"

"No, of course not," Nora was quick to reply. "It's our call, of course … Joint, like every other decision."

"So it is." He smiled to her. "Let's not talk about it right now. We have a whole year to decide. Doctor … what's his name, Patel? Doctor Patel will help us sort this out. Isn't that what therapists are for?"

"What if we don't like Doctor Patel?" Nora worried.

Michael was becoming testy.

"You know the DVP doesn't recommend alternates. It would make it look as if we're trying to hide something from the observers they pick. How hard could it be to adapt to a shrink? We've adapted to everything else."

Nora nodded, uncertain, but earnestly willing.

"You're right." She smiled. "Provider knows best."

She looked at the holofolder, thick with the contacts of people who would scrutinize their every weakness and their every strength for one full year.

"So this is where our taxes go," she mused. "All this bureaucracy ..."

"This is where our taxes should go. Not to another Stingdrone."

Nora laughed. "My dad would say I'm marrying a goddamn Communist."

Michael nodded. "I'll take that as a compliment. The Americans gave us a *lot* of great ideas, but *we* put them into practice. So now let them and the rest of the world give each other no end of grief with their obsolete priorities."

"Is it true that the DVP has hidden ethnic quotas when they grant the License?" Nora wondered. "That they favor ... I don't know, Designation Sverige over Designation Méhico?"

"Not true. In Oikonea Province, for instance, Designation Méhico is no longer a minority. In fact, the entire Designation Hispanic has one of the lowest deferment rates in the country."

Nora had grown tired of discussing the politics of the Republic.

"Mom and I picked the wedding dress," she said, taking a sip of her vintage Colawine.

"Can I see it before the wedding? Or are the ancient customs still in place in the Age of Rational Choice?"

"Still in place, and you can't see it," Nora said archly. "*Something* should be left to surprise, even in the Age of Rational Choice."

"You know who else just turned in their first application? Alan and Steve. They're getting married at the end of November, of course we're invited."

He took another bite of his corndog. "Did I ever tell you that Steve's first name is not actually Steve?" he said then.

Nora was surprised. "I didn't know that. He changed it? Why?"

"Interesting story," Michael answered with a grin. "You remember that phrase *'God created Adam and Eve, not Adam and Steve'*? They wanted their names to be a dig at the homophobes, so they made it Alan and Steve."

She laughed. "That's so funny … I like it. Is it Alan or Steve who will be keeping his wedding suit a surprise?" she asked with a good-natured chuckle.

"Alan, of course. They've already signed the contract with the certified maternal surrogate. I met their CMS. She seems like the right person."

"And the Reproductive Bank?"

"Genetic material from both. More expensive, but they believe in doing everything equally."

"And we don't?" Nora quipped. "I'm happy for them. They'll make good parents."

Michael put his hand on hers. "So will we."

Nora smiled to herself in the way of every woman when talking about her future with the man she loves. Like every woman, she couldn't wait.

*   *   *

Michael's boss and coworkers, Alan and Steve first among them, congratulated him on the engagement and the application, and wished him the best of luck in the marathon.

Michael took a week off work for the most immediate tasks of contacting the observers, going through his first medical exam, his lab work, and his first individual therapy session. His boss was required to treat all those days as regular paid working days, validated by the various observers. The employers too had a stake in the next generation; everybody did.

Nora had to take many more days off than her fiancé. As Dr. Canetti reminded her, a woman's reproductive system is so much more complicated than a man's, and her involvement in the life of her child so much more exhaustive. Nora was poked, prodded, injected, monitored, and asked a great deal of questions. All that extra attention made her unnervingly aware of how inflexibly her gender had been constructed to be in the service of the species.

Michael had needed less than ten minutes and a men's magazine in Dr. Canetti's bathroom; she had to lie flat in the stirrups for half an hour while latex-clad fingers and steel tools went into her. Michael "gave" his sperm; Nora's eggs had to be "extracted". There were times when it got to her.

Mom accompanied her to every visit. Ennie Savins had nothing against all sorts of specialists making sure that her daughter, her son-in-law and her grandchildren were well.

"But what's this about freezing genetic material at the reproductive bank?" she wanted to know.

"In case we keep being rejected … deferred … until our genetic material is no longer in its prime," Nora explained. "Fifth Law: *It takes an instant to become a parent, a lifetime to be one.*"

The Fifth Law had been added to the Constitution by Founding Mother Mariama Binti Dembele, an immigrant from Designation Senegal.

"I hope no one uses our genetic material for who knows what unholy purposes," Ennie worried.

Ennie was only mildly annoyed when she received the call from Dr. Patel, informing her that she and her husband were required to make an appointment with the generational psychologist for a first joint-therapy session.

"I guess the old way wasn't the whole story," she commented philosophically. "All we were ever told about grandkids was that we should spoil them rotten."

Her husband Nick was beyond annoyed.

"We're becoming a nation of goddamn shrinks," he fumed. "A platoon of so-called experts telling us what to do. Since when does a man need to be taught how to love his own flesh and blood?"

"That's not the point, Dad." Nora interjected. "One needs to be taught how to *implement* love."

"What a crapload of bullshit. Now it's you sounding like a goddamn shrink. It has become harder in this country to have children than it was for me to get into the American military first, and into our military then."

"Better this than making an easy mess of our own flesh and blood," Ennie countered, "even despite our best intentions."

"And now, by way of 'progress', we've got the government acting as both Mommy and Daddy," Nick insisted. "Nurturance on one side, enforcement on the other, and everything tied up into one hell of a knot."

"The first available date is next Wednesday," Ennie silenced him. "I'll lay out the burgundy shirt for you."

Nora put her arms around her father's shoulders. She thought about Michael, whose parents had died in a car crash when he was twenty-two. Easier for him on that count, too, she thought. Michael didn't have to deal with a previous generation reluctant to be scrutinized by a platoon of experts. Then right away, she regretted her thought.

"What happens if I refuse to see the shrink?" Nick asked belligerently.

Nora placed a dinner plate in front of him. "In that case, they'll ask you to sign a statement to the effect that you refused generational therapy."

"So they can blame Grandpa if the kid's screwed up?" Nick shouted. "This is outrageous!"

"Calm down and eat your matsutake loaf," Ennie said. "No one's going to blame Grandpa."

Dr. Patel was a short, overweight man in his forties with salt-and-pepper hair and a faint, but noticeable accent. His office was small, but cozy enough for the countless prospective parents who had gone in and out over the course of his twenty years of practice.

Almost an entire wall was taken up by mini-holographs of the smiling couples who had been granted their License with the help of his services. There was no visible mention anywhere in the mini-holographs of how many times each couple had applied, but some of those couples looked old enough to be grandparents instead of parents.

"Miss Savins, would you say you were loved by the right people in the right way for the right reasons and at the right time?" was his first question, shot the moment she took her seat.

"I beg your pardon?"

Dr. Patel smiled, seemingly smug at yet another first-time applicant he had taken aback.

"Forgive me, Miss Savins. I like to go to the core of the issue. That's the core of the issue, is it not? To have the best chance in life one must be loved by the right people in the right way for the right reasons and at the right time. Everything else is a corollary."

"Oh … Yes, I imagine so," Nora managed, rooting in her mind for the meaning of "*corollary*".

"You will be sent detailed notes from my parents' therapy," she said then. "Shouldn't that give you an idea of whether I was loved by the right people, etcetera, etcetera?"

Dr. Patel seemed to miss her veiled hostility. Or perhaps he had long learned not to show his clients that he had registered their hostility.

"In our individual sessions, I'm only interested in your individual opinion," he replied. "But you are right. Whenever possible, it takes a minimum of two generations to assess the damage."

Damage, Nora thought. He sounded like an insurance adjustor. She thought of Michael again. With no paternal grandparents to bring into the picture, and Michael being an only child, Dr. Patel would have to assess the damage based on Michael alone. Perhaps that was a point in Michael's disfavor, she worried.

After that startling beginning, the rest of the session had seemed only a bit easier to her. Dr. Patel audiotaped all sessions, as per required procedure, and videotaped them as well, if the patient consented. Nora had been advised that the videotape was sent for analysis to the body language experts. She told him she wanted no videotape; then right away she wondered whether her refusal could be used against her.

Perhaps defensively, she had nothing but good things to say about her parents. The length of their marriage alone seemed an argument in their favor and hers. But she was becoming more and more uncomfortable under Dr. Patel's gaze.

She caught herself looking out of the corner of her eyes, trying to guess where the tape recorder and the camera were hidden. The observers' intention in hiding both must have been to put the patients at ease and have them act spontaneously. Genius, she thought contemptuously, given that the patients knew they were being recorded. Her irritation was getting worse with every passing minute. And this was just the beginning, she worried. How would she make it to the finish line?

Before the end of the hour, Dr. Patel handed her a sheet of paper and told her to write down why she wanted to be a mother.

"First, pick one of these, please," he said, and lined up six writing implements on his desk.

There was a pencil with a sharp point, a pencil with a stubby point, a ballpoint pen, a laser pen, a silver fountain pen, and a red felt-tip marker. Nora's hand hovered over the desk. What, no quill?

Dr. Patel was looking at her steadily, registering her every twitch, no doubt with his peripheral vision as well. She picked up the ballpoint pen and glanced up to see if her choice met with his approval. Dr. Patel remained blank-faced. What a profession, she thought.

"Now, please write your answer," Dr. Patel said. "I'll let you finish at your own pace. I'll be in the next room."

Alone, Nora was free to shake her head and huff under her breath. Then she looked nervously around the office: could she be sure she wasn't being videotaped in secret? No, she reassured herself; recording patients in any way without their knowledge was against the law, of that she could be certain.

Finally, she had enough. She pulled the sheet of paper to her and, under the line in caps that read, "Why I want to be a mother", she put down all the buzzwords she thought Dr. Patel must be looking for: "personal legacy", "biological fulfillment", "emotional rewards", "gift of love", "service to the country", and "duty to the species".

Dr. Patel came back some five minutes later, with his unflappable smile.

"Here," Nora said, handing him the sheet of paper.

Without looking at it, Dr. Patel quickly slipped it into his desk drawer.

"Thank you. I don't keep this, you know. It goes to the graphology experts. That's another requirement."

"Ah," Nora said.

She wanted to ask whether the choice of writing implement computed into the graphology test, but she knew the answer.

"I'll see you at our next appointment," Dr. Patel said amiably.

"All right. Thank you, Doctor."

By the time she left the office, she was beginning to feel like a lab rat in a neurobiologist's nightmare.

Around that time, Michael was still asleep in his cubicle, the soundproof retractable screens cushioning him from the noise and the lights of the floor where he worked.

There had been no end of protests from employers when the nap hour had been introduced. This wasn't Italia, with its afternoon siestas, they'd argued, and it wasn't Nihon, with its morning calisthenics. Then, in a few short weeks, productivity had increased, traffic accidents had decreased, and resistance had been swept aside.

What was Michael dreaming about? She wondered whether they were the same sort of dreams she had, and whether he would recount them at his next therapy session — behind her back, she thought, with a streak of bitterness.

But there were the preparations for the wedding to keep her happily distracted. There was the dress to be fitted, the cake to be picked, the invitations to be sent — that, at least, hadn't changed. The old customs had also been reintroduced of the bride bringing a trousseau, and the groom what used to be called a bride price. The latter, however, smacked of the time when women were tradeable commodities, and was now called "husbandly contribution".

"Thanks to the introduction of the Parenthood Laws," the media were fond of saying, "marriage is once again the 'big deal' it was always meant to be. Marriage is, first of all, a proper merger, a contract between families creating a united front for the good of the next generation. No two citizens are more thoughtless than the couple who elopes for the quick and squalid trip to Reno."

"That's me and you, Ennie," Nick Savins grumbled. "Thoughtless and squalid to the core. A few years down the line, they'll abolish divorce, and then we'll make it full circle back to the Dark Ages."

Michael had survived his intake therapy session with ease.

"It's like the first cut into old paint," he shrugged, "so you can get started on the stripping." Michael loved to work around the house, and he was very good at it.

Nora burst into a jovial laugh. "I don't even want to know how many layers of old paint need to be stripped in your case," she joked.

Truth be told, with the start of those separate sessions, an unpleasant curiosity had begun to eat at her. What was Michael telling Dr. Patel? she wondered, and why was Michael so much more comfortable with having his layers of paint, as he put it, stripped?

"Did the good doctor make you write that Why and Wherefore nonsense?" she asked him.

Couples were not allowed to discuss their individual sessions outside of the observers' office, and that was another thing that bothered Nora. In a fit of rebellion, she had decided to break that one rule, and had mentioned to Michael the "Why I want to be a parent" requirement.

"Oh that," Michael replied, rolling his eyes. "With the choice of writing implements and all … Yes, he made me write that nonsense. I gave him all the answers you told me you gave him, only scrambling the order of appearance of the phrases, and using every synonym I could think of. He may have caught on, but of course he didn't tell me."

"I bet he did catch on," Nora said. "The man's a human sponge … If he did, I personally don't care."

"Can't blame you," Michael said. He made a gesture of annoyance. "What did Dr. Patel expect me to say that you didn't say too? '*I want to be a parent because it's fashionable?*'"

"That's my son-in-law," Nick praised him. "You tell these well-intentioned idiots."

Four weeks later, all was ready for the big day. The wedding, at sunset on the lakeshore under the reddening maples, came off without a hitch. Nick and Ennie had spared no expenses, and Michael had brought a handsome contribution in cash. Nora's sister Jillian was a graceful maid of honor, Michael's cousin Thierry was a witty best man.

"I'd like to conclude with some wise words from a golden age past," Thierry said at the end of his speech. "It's from an American song, but we do owe the Americans so much, for good and ill."

There was pleasant laughter from the guests.

"*First comes love, then comes marriage, then comes baby in a carriage.*" Thierry recited. "In that order, my friends. Love is already there, and, as everybody can see, it's the real thing. There is no doubt in my mind that baby will be next."

He turned to the couple and raised his glass of champagne.

"To Michael and Nora," he toasted, "and to Michael and Nora's License. I wish them from my heart that they will have to wait only three hundred and sixty-five days."

Applause and a chorus of, "Idem, idem," followed his words.

Nora laid her head on Michael's shoulder. She thought of the month that had passed, and of the months to come. It seemed like such a task. But it was worth it, she told herself. It was well worth it.

She raised her glass and mouthed the words, "Thank you."

THREE

D<small>R. C</small>ANETTI SWITCHED OFF HER MEDISCREENS and turned to face her two patients.

"It's a topic that must be addressed," she began. "And I don't believe in sweetening the pill … if you will allow me the most overused of medical puns." She had a kind, patient face, and she was easy to talk to.

Nora shot an anxious look at Michael sitting beside her. Michael didn't seem to be much more at ease, not this time.

"There is always the possibility that the child or children will have a disease or defect we can't prevent," Dr. Canetti explained. "Spina bifida, autism, progeria, the list goes on. We do our best to diagnose as early as possible, but medical knowledge is limited, and always will be."

She sighed. "Even with all our medical advances, I tell my patients that the moment they decide to become parents, their fingers get permanently stuck."

"How do you mean?" Michael inquired.

Dr. Canetti lifted one hand and put her middle finger over her index finger.

"Back in the days of superstition, this meant 'Let's hope all goes well.'"

Michael chuckled. "I don't see how putting one finger over the other would ensure that all goes well."

Dr. Canetti nodded. "Some things are scary in every century."

"And if the child has a … disease or defect?" Nora asked.

"Then you have the usual three options: abort, give the child up for adoption, or keep the child. If you decide to keep the child, you will be asked to sign a clause stating that you are willing to shoulder all the added parental responsibilities required by the disease or defect. Financial responsibilities, emotional responsibilities, commitment in terms of time and effort … and, of course, you need to keep in mind that, depending on the severity of the disease or defect, you might not be relieved of your parental responsibilities when the child reaches eighteen, as it happens with healthy offspring."

Nora seemed on the verge of tears, as if Dr. Canetti had just made that dreaded diagnosis.

"As for abortions, those recommended by a physician are covered by the National Insurance. Abortions not recommended by a physician come out of your pocket, and they are not cheap."

"And the reason?" Michael asked.

"The reason is to keep abortion from becoming a method of contraception."

"Fair enough," Michael agreed.

Dr. Canetti smiled. "Too soon to discuss this issue, right? I just wanted to make you aware of the rules and options."

"Yes, thank you," Michael said.

"Believe it or not," Dr. Canetti added, "the most common 'defect', if we can call it such, is that the human brain has become about six ounces heavier in both sexes. We believe it's a spontaneous evolutionary step developed in order to accommodate all the added information humans need to absorb nowadays, and to avoid cognitive overload. In the last few years, there has been also a slight enlargement of the finger pads, due to our constant use of buttons and keyboards."

"Wow," Nora said under her breath.

Dr. Canetti got up. "Shall I make our next appointment, then? How does the fifteenth sound?"

Michael switched on the Panta10 strapped to his wrist and scrolled down the screen crowded with appointments with what looked like a university's worth of certified observers.

"The fifteenth's good."

"I'll see you then," Dr. Canetti said.

"One question," Nora interjected. "What if both parents become incapacitated?"

"Then there's the old option of giving the minor child or children to their relatives, first choice to closest blood relatives. But relatives must be certified fit to raise the children. We have special applications for relatives."

"Of course," Nora muttered sarcastically to herself. "Why shouldn't applicant relatives be put under the microscope … And if the relatives don't pass muster?"

"The other old option, a certified adoptive home."

"All right. Thank you for all the information." Nora said.

Michael and Nora walked out of her office. The moment they were out, Nora let go of the angry tears she'd been trying to hold back.

"Michael, I can't take this anymore. Laws, rules, regulations, certifications, clauses … My head is swimming, I'm exhausted."

"I know, sweetie, I know. It's worse than being in college, tests and more tests ... But that's the point, you see? If we had to jump through all those hoops to get a college degree, it makes sense that we should jump through hoops to get something so much more important."

She pulled away from him and rooted in her purse for a tissue.

"You know? I've had enough of your acquiescence," she said between sniffles. "*Sounds good, Doctor. Sounds fine, Doctor. We'll do this, we'll do that.*"

He looked her squarely in the eyes.

"And what would you have me do?" he argued back. "Tell them, 'No, Doctor we won't do this' and 'No, Doctor we won't do that'? Do you want this baby, or don't you?"

Nora sat in the passenger seat and slammed the car door shut.

"Yeah, I want this baby. I'm just not sure I'll be sane by the time it's born."

*   *   *

They made the trip to her parents' home without another word on the subject.

The handsome house where Ennie and Nick Savins had lived for over twenty years bordered with an apple orchard and had undergone a thorough retrofitting, financed in part by the Department of Household Sustainability. Solar panels shone on the roof, as they did on the roof of every other house in the quiet cul-de-sac. A beautifully-kept kitchen garden was where the useless ornamental front lawn had once been.

Ennie and Nick had disagreed on the kitchen garden.

"Do we grow it organically?" Ennie had proposed.

"We grow it *scientifically*," Nick had replied. "Like they've been growing that apple orchard all the way back since the time of our first Madam President."

Eventually, Ennie had given up. Her only non-negotiable expenses were the composting bin and the wind-powered incinerator.

Michael and Nora, still silent and not looking at each other, stepped on the porch and rang the bell.

From behind the door, they heard a steady, convulsed wail, like a car alarm for which the clicker had been lost. It took Ennie a while to answer the door. She was still in slippers and bathrobe, and she looked exhausted. From inside the house, barely audible under the screaming, Nick's rumbling voice came in a steady stream of swearwords.

"He has finally agreed to see the generational therapist with me," Ennie said, trying to smooth her hair with her hands. "So, they shipped us the baby while you were out. Two babies, in fact. Given that the gender choice hasn't been made yet, they said we'd get random selection. Congratulations, it's twin boys!" she added with a weak smile.

Michael and Nora walked into the den. Nick was awkwardly holding a newborn, who was naked, except for a diaper that was almost falling off. Lying flat on the sofa, a second newborn wailed in unison with the first — both small bodies shaking, fists pummeling the air, and faces the color of wrinkled pomegranates.

On the kitchen table, and on the end tables, were piled-up boxes of diapers, wipes, ointment, formula, clothes, booties, blankets, pacifiers, toys — the whole mind-numbing mountain of stuff needed for a newborn — and everything in duplicate. Still to come from the Department of Vital Privileges were a double crib, a double bassinet, a double car seat, a double stroller, a double high chair, two body slings, a bathing tub, a changing table, and a room monitor.

Everything was made mostly of plastic. Nothing better had yet been found to substitute that traditional cheap, lightweight, waterproof, and unbreakable material. Also, the environmental experts had long ago calculated that dumping into landfills tons of disposable diapers was no less environmentally unsound than using up very scarce water to wash tons of cloth diapers. The Republic had strict laws designed to curb carbon footprints, but the biggest carbon footprints were those created by its smallest citizens.

"We're being punished," Nick was yelling. "It's goddamn unfair!"

"Be quiet, Nick," Ennie snapped. "It could have been triplets, quadruplets, who knows. Just keep holding his head ... His *head*, Nick!"

Nora was too upset to look at the two robots.

"HumaNew babies," the media touted them, "are a marvel of North Korean technology in the service of applicant parents, the closest thing to a real baby ever invented."

And indeed, one never knew at what point a HumaNew baby would pee, poop, throw up, get hungry, get full, get hot, get cold, get sick, get frightened, roll to the edge of a changing table, or cry for no discernible reason, as Nick and Ennie's grandchildren had been doing on and off for almost half an hour.

The babies, and the baby supplies, were on loan from the DVP. If the application was granted, the babies were returned to the DVP, while the supplies became the property of the applicant parents, who were required to pay only for the diapers and the baby food used up in the past year.

Damaging the babies brought a fine equal to the cost of repairing them. As yet another lesson in personal responsibility, the fine was to be paid by the applicant parents, regardless of whether it had been they or others who had done the damage, and regardless of whether the damage had been done intentionally or not. So, for a host of reasons, the HumaNews were treated with even more care than real new humans.

The concept was not a novel one. Teenagers in America were given ten-pound sacks of flour to keep for a month as stand-ins for infants, in an attempt to deter them from pregnancy. Comedians had been kept busy mining jokes from the flour-sack babies, until robotics applied to the Parenthood Laws had taken the idea to an entirely new level.

Michael craned his neck over first one, then the other twin. There was physical hurt in the way the crying slammed onto his eardrums. Like every parent everywhere, he wondered how such a tiny creature could produce such an astonishing sound.

According to the experts, "The disproportionate noise is the evolutionary way of ensuring that helpless human infants can attract the adults' attention to their needs. The unsolvable evolutionary glitch is that human infants are able to attract the adults' attention, but unable to indicate the need to which the adults' attention is to be directed."

Nick dropped the baby next to his brother and went to get a third cup of black syncaf. Ennie quickly stepped in to move the babies, so they wouldn't suffocate under the sofa cushions. As she moved the baby who hadn't been diapered yet, the baby shot up a stream of yellow liquid that hit her in the face.

"Well," she commented, reaching for the wipes. "I had daughters, how was I supposed to anticipate this?"

"Is it my imagination, or do they look a bit like me and Nora?" Michael wondered with a puzzled frown.

"Oh, they do look like the two of you, all right," Ennie replied. "The DVP people make a personalized microchip out of your ID holograms. They take the parents' features and blend them into one. Isn't that clever?"

"Why would they do that?" Michael asked.

"The user's manual says it's to facilitate bonding and attachment," Ennie explained. "They reprogram the resemblance for every new set of applicant parents. It's uncanny, really," she added, with a look that was at once awed and alarmed.

"It's still a goddamn machine," Nick shouted over the babies' crying. "How in the hell am I supposed to bond with a goddamn machine? If they were my real grandchildren, I'd become attached in a New York heartbeat, as they used to say."

For no reason that could be determined, all of a sudden both babies stopped crying.

"About time!" Nick almost shouted.

"Shhhh," Ennie said.

"What should we name the little darlings?" Nick asked, looking at them askance.

"How about Dave and Don?" Ennie proposed. "No, Davy and Donny."

"Davy and Donny sounds good," Michael agreed.

"Dumb and Dumber sounds better," Nick muttered.

"Then it's Davy and Donny," Ennie concluded. "I guess we'll toss a coin to see which baby goes with which name."

Nora had disappeared into what had been her room. She sat on the rocking chair, holding her old doll against her chest.

So this was the "service to the new generation" everybody praised as the highest good. More like slavery to the next generation, she thought grimly. She looked around at the room where she'd spent so many years without a thought for the next generation, and the tears came back.

Ennie peeked in. "Sweetheart? Are you all right?"

"I'm not sure, Mom. I was thinking I'm too young to start missing my childhood."

Ennie sat next to her.

"Oh sweetie, I know."

"How was it with me and Jillian?" Nora asked. "Did you and Dad reach the point where you wished you hadn't had us?"

"Never. But we had to learn everything on the job, with no one to tell us how to do it. We had to live with our mistakes, too. Your father calls them retroactive nightmares … Like that time he forgot he had to pick Jillian up and she had to wait for him almost half an hour in an empty schoolyard. Every time he thinks about it, he still cringes … and so do I, although I have certainly created a few retroactive nightmares of my own."

Nora's memory went back to one of her therapy sessions.

"The only useful thing Dr. Patel told me so far is that, unless everyone can be programmed to do everything right, all parents are bound to hurt their children unintentionally."

She chuckled. "I bet Dr. Patel wishes he could discover how to program everyone to do everything right. Our grateful nation would give him the Spock Prize for Peace thru Rational Choice."

Ennie hugged her. "It's better this way, believe me. You get to do your internship first. You get to make fewer mistakes."

"Do we, really?"

"Well, you know how every parent will tell you that the second child raises itself? That's true in so many ways … After one goes through a HumaNew, every first child may very well be the second."

Nora put her arms around her mother and sniffled away the last of her tears.

"How did it go this morning with Dr. Canetti?" Ennie asked.

"We talked about the disease or defect clause. I don't even want to think about that … You know something, Mom? I have a suspicion that this disease or defect clause is the DVP's way of discouraging the parents from bringing those children into the world."

"You mean some sort of … eugenics?"

"Huh-huh."

"Terrifying thought," Ennie said under her breath.

Nora shook her head. "Who knows in what other ways we're being manipulated without our knowledge ..."

"And the paternal options?"

"Michael refused to wear an empathy belly, and to be present at the delivery."

"Did he say why?"

"He said he doesn't need an empathy belly to understand what a pregnant woman goes through, because all he has to do is look at the nine-month patients in the waiting room."

"Yep, that should do it," Ennie mused. "And the delivery room?"

"That was less clear-cut. He said it's not his place to be in the delivery room ... He says it's obscene that the father should be underfoot with a camera zoomed in."

"And what do you think?"

"I agree. I'm not in love with the idea of a camera zoomed in, either."

She looked at her mother. "Dad was there for you with both of us, wasn't he?"

Ennie made a small shrug. "To be honest, I didn't want him around before or during the deliveries. As for after ... let's just say it was me breastfeeding at three in the morning, while he participated by snoring in the guest room."

"In retrospect," she added, "that was only fair. He was the one who had to wake up at five a.m. every morning to report to the barracks. He was the provider ... and a good one, too."

From outside the bedroom came the voices of the two men trying to shush the babies. Nick was shouting, "Shut up, you goddamn monsters!"

Ennie and Nora stifled a laugh. Then Nora got up from her rocking chair. She saw herself sitting in that chair with her baby in her arms, and all the challenges she and Michael still had ahead of them seemed again worth the trouble.

"Let's go before he has a stroke," Ennie said. "Are you and Michael staying for dinner?"

"I'll ask him. Mom?"

"What, sweetheart?"

"Thank you for persuading Dad to go see the therapist. That's one less thing we have to worry about."

"Sure, sweetie. If you ask me, he should have started seeing a therapist at age ten. Let's go now."

"And if the new humans don't stop crying?"

"Well, if you want my non-certified opinion: first, we make sure they're fed and changed, not too hot and not too cold, not too lonely and not too crowded, and then, if all of that checks out, we let them scream their little hearts out until they fall asleep."

Nora laughed. "And if they don't fall asleep?"

"Nothing a hammer can't fix."

*   *   *

"All right," Dr. Patel began, settling into his chair. "Let's address the gender choice, and let's do it systematically and rationally."

"Not that we would be allowed to do it otherwise," Nora quipped.

Dr. Patel ignored the barb.

"Let's start with you, Michael. Since you have expressed a preference for a boy as your firstborn, please tell Nora what you feel are the advantages of you and Nora being the parents of a firstborn boy."

Michael cleared his throat, then shook his head with an awkward smile.

"You're not going to like my arguments, Doctor. I have the feeling you'll find them prehistoric."

Dr. Patel made the conciliatory gesture of opening his hands.

"I'm here to help you both sort out your feelings, not to judge them. Please go ahead … and, of course, be as honest as possible, first of all with yourself."

Michael tried to buy time with another pause.

"Here's the thing," he said at last. "No matter what I hear in the media and on the job and everywhere else, this is still a man's world — and I think it's always going to be. You know … I figure you don't have to tell a son not to go to the raze party or walk alone in the tree belt at night or accept a drink from a stranger. I'd have to tell him to turn off the holoscreen while he's driving, to be home at a certain hour, all of that … But with a daughter, I'd have to tell her all of that *and* I'd have to tell her also not to go to the raze party or walk alone in the tree belt at night or have drinks with a stranger … ."

He looked first at Nora, then at Dr. Patel. "Am I totally off the mark here?"

Dr. Patel nodded to Michael to indicate that he had heard his opinion, then addressed Nora.

"Argument to the contrary?"

Nora eyed Michael with a bit of a sarcastic smile.

"Argument to the contrary, our daughter will start taking lessons in Shaolin kung fu at age six, like my sister and I did."

Michael dropped his head.

"True, daughters need to be taught caution," Nora went on. "Take rape, of course … You have to teach a daughter not to become a rape victim, but you also have to teach a son not to become a rapist. Same thing for an unauthorized pregnancy. A daughter may be the one who comes home pregnant, but a son may be the one who comes home having initiated the unauthorized pregnancy. Am *I* totally off the mark?"

Michael made no comment. There was a long pause. Then he pulled himself up, looking not at Nora, but at Dr. Patel.

"All right, let me come clean here. How am I going to explain why I think that I would be able to love a firstborn son better than a firstborn daughter?" He sounded slightly panicked. "I mean … at the emotional level, beyond the rational considerations?"

He turned to Nora with a pleading look. "I just *know* I want a boy, that's all."

"And I just know I want a girl …" Nora whispered, her face averted.

"How about boy and girl twins?" she asked Dr. Patel.

Dr. Patel made a slightly unconvincing nod.

"That is an option, of course. Some applicant parents solve the problem that way. You do know, however, that a choice of twins requires a double concurrent application. Double effort, double commitment, double time …"

"Yeah," Michael said with a grin. "We've got twins at home right now. It's double everything, all right."

There was another long pause. Nora was rubbing her hands together with a gesture of distress.

"It seems that we haven't come to a solution today," Dr. Patel said, looking at his clock. "We'll have to resume where we left off. But remember, you have ample time to make your gender choice. You can fill in the preference box the day before your year expires."

Michael nodded tiredly. "All right. We'll see what happens between now and then." He opened the door for Nora and walked out of the office with her.

"We probably could —" she began.

"Please, Nora, that's enough," he cut her off. "You know what? Fine, let's make it a girl. And the boy is Application Two."

"But you must *really* want it," Nora begged.

"Oh sweetheart," Michael said, "I don't even *know* what I really want anymore."

FOUR

TWO WEEKS LATER, when Nora went back to school, she
found trouble brewing in her senior class.

It was Marina Tafwe, the seventeen-year-old transfer. Marina
had been suspended again on disciplinary charges, and this time
she'd hinted to one of her classmates that she was going to run
away and have a baby with her boyfriend — or with any man
who came along.

It was a common threat made by teenagers to frighten their
parents, who were held responsible for their minor children's
unauthorized pregnancies; but Marina Tafwe was not the sort of
girl who made empty threats.

At the end of the class Nora stopped her student before she
left.

"Marina, I need to talk to you in my office," she said.

Marina looked at her with undisguised hostility.

She was pasty-faced, and chubby for her age. Her silver top and faded slacks were so tight every roll and dip of her body showed, making her look even heavier. She'd never made it past a C5 average, and she cheated every chance she got. Nora thought of her as living proof that, even with their best efforts, the observers still let a worrisome number of parents slip through the net.

Marina turned off her tablet. The latest school model was no thicker than a doubled-up X-ray film.

"What do we need to talk about?" she said sullenly.

Nora didn't let the girl's disrespectful manner discourage her.

"Something important," she answered.

She walked down the hallway to her office, let Marina go in first, then closed the door.

"I didn't cheat this time, Miss Savins," Marina said.

"Mrs. Holmes," Nora corrected her. "I know you didn't cheat. This is about something else. Sit down."

Marina squeezed into the chair and brushed a plaited dedlock away from her face. Nora thought dedlocks were the most unbecoming hairstyle ever invented, with an equally unbecoming name coined by teenagers who thought of themselves as dead in the water.

"Prilee told me —" Nora began.

"Prilee's a pain, okay?" Marina interrupted her. "She's jealous of me because she's a boondog."

"She's a what?"

"She's *ugly*. Like that dog they spliced with a baboon."

Nora sighed. Someone should compile a dictionary of teenagerese and shelve it in libraries next to the *Encyclopedia Britannica*, she thought.

"What did Prilee tell you this time?" Marina asked, almost glaring. "About me running away? Well, she's right, okay?"

Nora raised her hand to stop her.

"Prilee worries about you. For real, and you know that."

"Yeah, for real," Marina smirked. "Like my parents, like the observers …" She stopped in time not to add, "like you."

Well, Nora thought, it was true that she didn't really worry about Marina. She'd always felt an intense dislike for the girl and for her parents. All Nora worried about was that she didn't want to be the teacher whose student broke the First Law of the Republic.

The reason she'd taken Marina to her office, instead of sending her to Principal Meyer's office, was because it was always possible that someday Nora would have to talk a daughter of her own out of that sort of trouble. In fact, she thought, if she could persuade Marina to change her mind, she might get points with Dr. Patel. She found something deeply unsettling in that ironclad set of hierarchies.

"Why do you want a baby?" Nora asked then, and she realized that she was asking a seventeen-year-old the same question Dr. Patel had asked her.

Marina looked away.

"I don't have to answer that, okay?" she muttered.

She was silent for a long minute. At times her face seemed to be losing that anger pressed down tight in her chest. She was just a scared child, Nora thought, lashing out at the world with the only weapon she thought she had.

"I hate my parents, okay?" Marina finally blurted out, and Nora thought she wanted a sheindlin for every time she'd heard that. "They chew on me, they treat me like garbage … I hate my mother most of all, okay? She doesn't give a … she couldn't care less about me, I know she doesn't, even with all of her yapping …" Marina sniffled hard.

"But a baby at your age … You do know the consequences, right?"

"Yeah, like an automatic deferment on my first application means anything to me after I'll have my baby. Or the stupid fines and the stupid probation and the stupid community service and extra classes and everything else ... They can't take the baby away from me, can they?"

Nora shook her head. "Not anymore."

"You mean they used to?!"

"At the very beginning, so they tell me, until it was declared disproportionate punishment."

"Bonzer, mate," Marina scoffed. The latest teenage fad was all things Down Under. "And it would have defeated the purpose, huh?"

Nora motioned she didn't understand.

"Of giving the child the best start in life. Better a seventeen-year-old single mother and her cruddy parents than a foster home."

"Yes, I'd say you're right," Nora nodded. Marina wasn't all that stupid, she thought.

"What about GS?" Nora insisted.

"Yeah," Marina mocked. "Gin and Soda."

Nora ignored the sarcasm. "Guilt and Shame," she said flatly. "You would have to live the rest of your life knowing that you ruined the chances for your child ... And then what are you going to tell your child when your child asks you why you ruined its chances?"

Marina shifted uncomfortably in her chair. For a moment, it seemed that Nora's argument had broken through. There was another long silence.

"I just want ... I just want to show my mother, okay?" Marina finally blurted out.

"Show her what?"

"That I can be better than her ... That I can love my child ... *the right way for the right reasons at the right time,*" she recited with a contemptuous curl of her lips.

"Well, then, having a baby now is definitely not the right way, the right reasons, or the right time, is it?"

Marina tossed her dedlocks again.

"Yeah, well ... I'm sick and tired of all these shrinks telling me what to do, okay? I had to start at puberty, like everybody else ... My first pack of tampons, my first box of contraceptives, and my first appointment with a pregnancy prevention counselor. And the *educational shows* ..." she added, rolling her eyes.

The old American TV shows Nora too had had to sit through at Marina's age. *I'm sixteen, which one of these three men is my baby's father?* Or *I'm going to prove that you owe me five years' worth of child support.* Decades of that daily fodder, until having a baby had become as casual as having a burger.

In foreign countries, there was an entire separate category of citizens: unmarried parents called "baby mothers", or worse, "baby mamas"; and "baby fathers", or worse, "baby daddies". In the Republic, both appellations were one of the worst names someone could be called.

"You said you want to show your mother," Nora tried again. "Are you sure it's not because ... because you want to be like her?"

An instant later, she wondered where she'd fished out that question. Most probably from her own pregnancy prevention counselor, ten years before.

"Like my mother?" the girl sneered. "Why would I want to be like my mother?"

"So you can be a mother yourself ..." Nora groped. "Have what she has. Her ... power, her authority."

Marina looked at Nora as if Nora were a complete fool. She started to say something, shook her head, then locked herself into her stubborn silence again.

Nora understood the conversation had come to an end. Whether Nora had hit a nerve or not, Marina showed no signs of wanting to continue.

"Can I go now, Mrs. Holmes?" the girl begged.

"Yes, you can go now."

"Are you going to send me to the principal's office?"

"No. But I *am* going to ask you to think about your future. Go to college, get a good job … You can use the waiting time to take the classes, find a suitable man to marry …"

"I already have a man, okay? And he loves me enough to give me a baby."

"Does he love you enough to provide for you and your baby *after* he gives you a baby?" Nora rebutted. "Or do you want to be a baby mama?" She used the insult as her last resort.

Marina set her teeth. "We'll manage."

Nora winced. She wondered how many times Marina had been asked the same reasonable questions by her parents, her counselors, her doctors, and how many times Marina had given all of them the same unreasonable answers.

All those ancient catchphrases came back to her mind: *Be cool, stay in school,* and the rest. Since when had a teenager been stopped by catchphrases or educational shows? She wouldn't be surprised if Marina went into a fake marriage with this man of hers, even though, when it came to such arrangements, the Department of Vital Privileges was as strict as the Department of Human Intake.

"Oh honey, believe me, a child is not the sort of thing you can leave to chance," Nora said, switching to a softer approach. "I have two HumaNew babies at home, I know what I'm talking about."

Marina stared at the wall.

"Oh my God, the HumaNuisances," she groaned. "I had one last year."

"Did it look like you?"

"Why would it look like me?" Marina scoffed. "It's an ugly old thing … We all get these ugly old things."

Nora didn't reply. Of course, the DVP wouldn't give minors HumaNew babies bearing the parents' features, she thought. The last thing the DVP wanted was for teenagers to find anything appealing about *their* HumaNew babies.

"Look," Nora tried for the last time. "I just want you to think about it, that's all. Talk about it with your parents, your observers … I know you're mature enough to wait."

She spoke that last sentence while remembering the gesture of crossing one's fingers that Dr. Canetti had demonstrated for her.

Marina only made a small shrug.

"I'll see you in class tomorrow," Nora dismissed her.

She watched the girl get up and leave. Something her mother had said came back to her mind, something about making an easy mess of one's own flesh and blood in spite of every best intention.

So many kinks to be smoothed out, she thought; variables as old as the human race itself, as troubling as all the variables the species had fought since the beginning. Would they ever be tamed, she asked herself, those random chances that cared so little for the best intentions? She locked the door of her office and walked out.

As she was about to get on her bicycle, she heard loud shouting and angry noises coming from the other end of the street. It was another protest march. Above the crowd waved banners with, "End Reproductive Discrimination Now" and "We Don't Need An Observer's Grade To Be Grade-A Parents."

Who was enraged at the establishment this time, Nora wondered. The usual groups: college dropouts, new immigrants, workers from the argysium refinery. "Proletarians", they called themselves, and wasn't that a joke, she thought, given that the term had been coined in ancient Rome to describe the lowest-class members of society, who served the state only by producing offspring.

The media were never gentle on the proletarians, lambasted as irresponsible and lazy. With all the available student loans and state-sponsored facilitations, the argument went, how hard could it be to get a Level 2 Bachelor's degree? Even members of the military found time to complete the basic five-year program.

Nora was too tired to feel anything besides annoyance. With the marchers blocking the street, she would have to take an alternate route, and she would be home late. She was not a proletarian, but she had problems of her own. With or without the prospective of offspring, she thought, everybody in this brave new Republic had problems of their own.

*   *   *

Michael had been watching the twins all morning — battling them, rather. Nora refused to furnish or decorate the nursery until the baby came, so all the baby supplies had been shoved into the guest bedroom. Now one of the upstairs rooms was completely empty, while the other was packed with the twins' cribs and everything else, including wholesale boxes of diapers stored inside the two cribs. Nora called the room "the baby shop".

The DVP had sent the items accompanied by the usual cutesy holocard.

"A baby shower from the Department of Vital Privileges," the holocard read. "Congratulations, Michael and Nora!" The names of the applicant parents were added with an electronic stamp.

Miraculously, Davy and Donny had fallen asleep at last. The hardest thing, of course, was telling them apart. The first couple of days, Davy had been fed twice while Donny had been left hungry, and Donny had had his diaper changed while Davy's had reached full capacity. Finally Nora and Ennie had color-coded everything: red for Davy and green for Donny. There was no other way; they were identical twins, in fact, more like clones.

Michael was taking advantage of the lull by catching up with a work assignment. He'd never thought being attached at the hip to a Homnya computer could become a welcome thing. The last time he and Nora had finished a meal in peace seemed like a distant memory, and it was months since they'd gone for corndogs to The Iowa State Fair restaurant where they'd celebrated the turning in of their application. As for sex … Michael thought — and then decided not to think about sex.

A couple of evenings earlier, more or less drifting on his way from work, he'd driven past Sex Row, just outside the city limits. It was just a quiet suburb with every porch light on, nothing like the red-light districts throbbing with rock'n'riffraff music and tawdry laser displays.

No bouncers leaning from smoky dark doorways, no barkers shouting obscene invitations past strolling families. More than anything else, Sex Row reminded him of that American brothel near Las Vegas where he had spent a memorable night during his senior year.

Michael had always thought that one of the smartest things the Republic had accomplished was rein in male sexual demand, and to have accomplished it in the most civilized way possible, given that male sexual demand was social chaos by definition.

He looked at those inviting houses where sex was now simply a clean, well-regulated business transaction, and he wondered whether he wanted to jeopardize the health of his marriage for the sake of a quick anonymous release. It wasn't worth it, he told himself, and drove home to Nora.

The latest of their parenting classes had been on safety. The instructor had taken them to a room marked "The Moment They Learn To Crawl" and had asked them to walk around looking for hidden hazards. They'd guessed nine out of ten, missing the thorntree bonsai on the mantelpiece. The house didn't have a pool — no one could afford a pool now that water had become so scarce with global warming — but they were planning to get a dog. The dog was a separate lesson in itself, attended also by Ennie and Nick.

Nick, as always, was the odd man out. It was all he could do not to start an argument with the instructor.

"I raised two daughters, didn't I? They made it to the age of consent alive and well, didn't they?"

Michael raised his hand to ask the instructor whether they were allowed to hire a babysitter.

"Yes, of course," was the answer. "But you'll need to keep in mind that the DVP doesn't pay for it."

"The reason being?" Nora chimed in testily. "Babysitters are part and parcel of raising children."

The instructor registered her testiness and replied in a patronizing tone that irritated her even more.

"Because babysitters can be abused by parents looking to shunt their responsibilities onto others, Mrs. Holmes."

Nora didn't say anything. *Unbelievable,* she thought. These people had worked out *everything.*

So Michael and Nora called a certified babysitter and paid her seventy keanus to watch two robots for two hours. The moment Michael and Nora were out of the driveway, both babies promptly proceeded to come down with diarrhea. By the time

Michael and Nora got back home, the sitter was at the end of her rope.

Two days earlier, Ennie had found out that one of the boys had an undescended testicle, which had prompted an unforeseen visit to the pediatrician. Now it was time for a video call to the pediatrician for advice on how to treat the diarrhea.

"I have the feeling HumaNew babies are this country's most effective means of contraception," Nora wailed. "It never ends."

Ennie didn't believe in mincing words.

"No," she said. "It doesn't end until you end … and, if you ask me, that should be the Seventh Parenthood Law. The only thing that keeps you going, and the only thing these dumb machines can't inspire, is love."

Nick had been willy-nilly reading some of the manuals provided by the DVP. So far he'd made it to the chapter on The Evolutionary Psychology of Reproduction.

"Love is not the word these goddamn Evolutionary Psychologists would use. To them it's … listen to this: '*psycho-biological attachment to a future generation that perpetuates one's name and one's genes.*' Let's frame this beauty and hang it in the kid's room. Won't that make her feel special."

Ennie ignored him and patted Nora's hand.

"It's love all right," she told her gently. "Once that's in place, everything will be so much easier, you'll see. And Michael," she added, "love will come whether it's a girl or a boy, trust me."

Michael's friends, Alan and Steve, didn't seem to be having an easier time with their baby: a girl they'd named Anthus. Anthus was born with a slightly defective heart valve, requiring just the extra degree of attention needed to drive her parents to total exhaustion.

The newest addition to the social life of Mr. and Mrs. Holmes was the time they spent talking about their children with other applicants. The last time Alan and Steve had been in their classes, the topic of discussion had been, "What should a parent do when their six-year-old announces she wants a sex change?"

"Round robins for an hour," Steve said rolling his eyes, "and in the end, topic left open for next class."

"That sounds like a tough one," Michael agreed. "I'm sure we're all going to need a refresher course a few years down the line."

"What do we get at the end of these blessed classes?" Alan inquired.

"Pass or fail," Michael replied. "And a holochart full of certificates of completion."

"I heard they also send grades to the DVP," Steve said. "Eyes Only, of course."

Michael put down his cup of syncaf. "That's just a rumor. At least I hope so, the proletarians are convinced it's real. Grades are supposed to be illegal."

"Has there ever been an applicant couple who tried to bribe their way into a pass of any kind?" Alan wondered.

"I'm sure there must be," Michael said. "The world is full of idiots. But observers who fake a pass risk losing their licenses. It isn't worth it for anybody, really."

Alan let a few drops of formula fall onto the inside of his wrist. Still too hot, and Anthus was beginning to fuss.

"So you picked the gender?" he asked Nora.

Nora shot a quick look at Michael, as if checking his reaction.

"Girl," she said then.

"The vote was three to one," Michael said with an agreeable smile.

From the kitchen came Jillian's voice.

"Three to two, Mike. Remember, the aunt is also on the side of the Y chromosome."

"Thank you, Jillian," Michael called back. He motioned toward the golden retriever napping at his feet. "I did get to pick the gender of the dog, though," he added with the same mild smile. "The dog's a boy."

Nora got up to clear the table and said nothing.

The twins were asleep in their bassinets, away from the heat of the solar fireplace. She looked at them, with those eerily familiar features of theirs: her mouth, Michael's curve of the jaw. A month from now, they would be swapped with the crawling models, and then an entirely new round of training would begin.

Jillian, two years older than Nora, had chosen to continue her career, and had put aside for the time being all thoughts of marriage and children. She helped often with the twins; while the DVP discouraged babysitting by strangers, there was no law against parental responsibilities being shared with relatives and close friends. But the more Jillian got involved with the babies, the more she was convinced that motherhood wasn't for her.

There were times when Nora envied her sister. Jillian was the exception, a woman happy to live her life unburdened by a sense of duty to the species or a desire for a personal legacy. Besides, Neri, the man she was involved with, was going through a brutal divorce, and that meant, as per the Sixth Law, "*Don't bring them in until everything's clean.*"

"Neri and I aren't 'any moron'," Jillian liked to say, echoing the First Law. "We are morons with a conscience."

"And I'm a moron with an unlimited free supply of the male pill," Neri added.

"Looks like now that we're past eighteen, the Republic counts on a certain amount of hard-earned responsibility," Michael commented.

Nora wasn't convinced. "Mandatory maturity, my father calls it. He says it cuts down on the gonad police."

"Well, mandatory or not, all you have to do is remember the excesses of the past," Michael replied. "Remember that horrific story … when was it, two thousand and eight? No, two thousand

and nine. Listen to this. There was this single woman in America who already had six children and was raising them on food stamps, and her doctors go and put her on fertility drugs. True story."

Jillian shook her head. "And with the fertility drugs she proceeds to have *octuplets*. Octuplets! Fourteen children born to a single mother living on public assistance. The height of irresponsibility, on everybody's part."

"We have a strange relationship with America, don't we?" Michael mused. "Our mother country, and at the same time the country we rebelled against ..." He laughed. "Dr. Patel would say that's how all children find themselves."

"By the way," Neri said, "does anybody know what the original movie line was? I'm told it involves some twentieth-century cussword or other."

"Oh it does," Nora said with a laugh. "The original line was, *You need a license to drive, you need a license to fish, you need a license to own a dog, but any asshole can become a father.*"

Michael grinned. "So it was only the father, huh?" He scratched the dog's droopy ears. "Well, now I have two licenses out of four."

"Shouldn't the Founding Father be the scriptwriter who wrote the line?" he asked then. "Keanu only speaks it."

"They get credit in the Constitution," Neri said, "the scriptwriters, the director, and all the other actors." He chuckled. "But Keanu was a handsome son of a devil, *his* official portraits are much prettier."

"The one thing I never liked much is the movie's title," Michael said. "*Parenthood* ... I think it's ... what's the word? Lackluster."

From the kitchen came the smell of something good baking in the oven.

"Hey, Jillian?" Neri called out. "Are you making cinnamon buns?"

"Yep. Mother's recipe."

Neri laughed. "Not fair. We don't have time for a quickie."

Jillian peeked through the door, looking puzzled.

"What do you mean?"

"The evolutionary experts say the smell of cinnamon buns is the greatest aphrodisiac for a male."

"You've got to be kidding me," Jillian wondered. "Any reason why?"

"None known," Neri said. "I think maybe it has to do with that old saying about the way to a man's heart going through his stomach."

"What about women?" Nora asked. "What's the greatest female aphrodisiac for us?"

Neri had a way of making others aware of how much he knew, sometimes to the point of being pompous.

"Baby powder," he said, with a smile full of meaning. "That doesn't need to be interpreted, does it?"

Nora poked Michael's side with her elbow and laughed.

"No wonder you're horny all the time."

"That sounds like a load of barfage" Michael countered. "There were no cinnamon buns or baby powder for Neanderthal or Cro Magnon. Their aphrodisiacs must have been a whole different story."

"You're right," Nora agreed. "And no baby powder or cinnamon buns for Aboriginal Peoples before contact ..." She shook her head. "That ought to tell you how much the EPs know."

"But the tug is universal," Jillian said from the kitchen.

Now it was Neri who seemed confused. Jillian wiped her hands on a towel and came to sit with the others in the den.

"That's what I call it, I don't know if the EPs have a name for it. You know those images where a man holds a baby in his arms? Preferably a well-muscled man without his shirt on?"

"I've seen those," Nora chimed in.

Jillian put her closed fist against her belly. "Gets a woman right here."

Neri gestured all around with his chin raised, imitating the instructor of a parenting class.

"Anyone for an answer to *this* evolutionary conundrum?"

Nora raised her hand, going with the joke. "Me, me, me!"

"Yes, our applicant mother." Neri nodded.

"Strong and tender male as provider and protector," Nora answered. She looked at Michael with a chuckle. "That would be you, honey."

Neri grinned. "Ding ding ding. Give the student an 'A'."

"That's why that stuff gets even women who don't want children," Jillian said. "You never outgrow the need to feel that everything's all taken care of."

"Wow," Michael said. "That sounds like the kind of copywriting that would go perfectly with the image."

"That's where I got it, "Jillian replied. "It was an old advert for an insurance company. The idea was to push your emotional buttons."

"I would imagine the tug gets men, too," Neri said. "I wouldn't mind being seen as the strong, yet tender … what was it? Proactive provider?"

"Proactive protector," Michael jokingly corrected him.

"It's even more effective if the male in the image is in uniform," Jillian said. "You know the old saying about all girls loving a man in uniform."

"Mother went for the soldier," Nora chuckled.

"And so many women who fall for their doctors," Jillian added. "A lab coat does the trick as nicely as any uniform ... males *specialized* in saving the lives of your offspring."

"And the 'bad boy'?" Nora inquired. "Does he belong in the same category?"

"Maybe not tender, but certainly a better protector than the wimp," Neri opined. He put up his fists and waved them in the air.

"Ain't none of y'all messin' with mah woman," he growled in a Texas baritone.

"Here come the cinnamon buns," Jillian announced. "No indecent behavior from the bad boys in the room, please."

The year had begun well, with two out of three of Michael and Nora's parenting classes passed without trouble. Individual therapy was more of a job.

The issue of gender preference kept coming up, and it didn't take Dr. Patel to see that it had become the most serious stumbling block. Michael had agreed on a girl, but only to please Nora. Nobody liked that concession made only to please Nora, but nobody had a better alternative.

The option of twin boy and girl had been abandoned almost immediately. Michael and Nora had made some thorough calculations and had arrived at the conclusion that, as their finances stood at the moment, they could not afford two children at the same time.

At the end of a particularly difficult session with Dr. Patel, Nora called her father, unbeknownst to Michael. It took her an effort to start the conversation, but she was reaching a breaking point.

"Dad, I need you to be honest with me ... Absolutely honest, promise me?"

"If I can help," Nick said unconvincingly, in fact, sounding alarmed.

When it came to baring his soul, Nick Savins wasn't much of a talker, as his wife and daughters knew well, and some topics were simply taboo with him.

"I need to ask you something, Dad," Nora began tentatively. "I need to ask … Did you ever wish you had a son? After Jillian and me, or … or *instead* of either Jillian or me?"

At the other end of the line, Nick made a sound of repressed anger.

"Why do they have to make everything so goddamn hard for everybody?" he said between his teeth. There was a long pause.

"I love you, Nora," he said then, "but I'm not going to dignify that with an answer. I'm only going to say one thing, and it's not as if we never talked about it before. Your mother almost died when she gave birth to you. After that, she couldn't have any more children. We knew that, and we accepted that."

His voice softened. "Your mother and I are more than happy with two daughters. We've been happy with you and with Jillian for twenty-eight years, and we will be happy with you and with Jillian for however many more years your mother and I have left."

There was another long silence. "Screw these doctors playing God. Potluck, Nora … When it comes to your children's gender, it's been potluck for millions of years, and that's the way it should be."

Nora was fighting tears. She didn't know why she felt so sad. Nothing her father had said had allayed her doubts. She had the feeling he was hiding something from her, giving her the pat answer he thought she wanted.

He was right, she told herself: it had been so much easier when the gender choice was impossible. Some things should be left to random chance; some outcomes should be accepted without question.

"All right, Dad," she finally said. "Thank you."

"Wait," Nick stopped her. "Have I made things a bit easier for you?" He sounded eager and worried at the same time.

"Yes, Dad," Nora lied. "Listen, can you and Mom watch the twins Saturday? Michael and I really need a couple of hours to ourselves."

"All right, sure."

"You know they've learned to crawl, right?"

"Yeah, I know. But no way in Satan's red hell I'm going to childproof my den for a couple of goddamn machines."

Nora laughed. "How's the therapy going?"

Nick made a snorting sound.

"It's going fine," he replied gruffly. "Not as useless as I thought. Found out a couple of things about your mother I wouldn't have found out in a thousand years … I can hold them against her forever now."

Nora couldn't help laughing.

"No doubt she can say the same thing about you … Thanks, Dad. I'll see you Saturday then."

"I'll see you Saturday, sweetheart."

*   *   *

When she returned to school the following Monday, she found unexpected news in the principal's office.

"It seems that during the latest proletarians' march, Marina's boyfriend was arrested for assaulting a police officer," Principal Meyer informed her. "So now he'll be spending a good chunk of his time in prison."

Nora's first reaction was relief.

"Let's hope Marina will use the fond absence from her Prince Charming to forget him," she sighed.

Principal Meyer shook his head.

"More likely she'll waste no time hooking up with another unlicensed male," he worried.

Nora left the office with the bad feeling that always came whenever the girl was mentioned. Never, she swore, would she and Michael end up with a daughter like Marina. In a way, she was grateful to the girl. Her most troublesome student had given her a real-life lesson that no parenting class could have provided.

FIVE

"LOOK, MICHAEL, WE'RE STILL IN TIME to turn in that second application for boy and girl twins. God knows we've got over six months' worth of experience already."

Michael had come to dread the topic. His face took on that vexed expression Nora had come to dread for her part.

"With the supplies from the DVP, we should make it through the first year," she added. "I'm sure we have enough for diapers and food."

"And after the first year?" Michael replied. "We have already agreed that we can't afford two children right now. Whereas by the time child number one is a few years old, I'll be making enough money to afford child number two."

"But my parents are more than willing to help us with the expenses," Nora tried again.

Michael didn't just look vexed; he looked downright unhappy.

"You know how I feel about being indebted to your parents. I've got nothing personal against them — you know I don't. I'm just against the idea of being indebted to *anybody*. I wouldn't have wanted to be indebted to my parents for that matter."

"Why do you have to be so stubborn?" Nora said in exasperation, and, once again, the subject dropped into an uncomfortable void.

There seemed to be nowhere else for her to turn except her mother; Ennie Savins didn't believe in taboo topics. On their way home from a shopping trip downtown, Nora took her to an open-air café and brought up with her the conversation that had been left hanging with her father.

"Did he, Mom? Did he ever tell you he wanted a boy?"

Ennie waved to the server for a refill of her cup of syncaf and sighed.

"All right. If you must know, he did tell me."

"I knew it," Nora whispered. "He's not a very good liar, is he?"

"And getting worse with age. You know, Nora, you're a grown woman, so let me cut to the chase. He's the last of his line, his name dies with him. It means a lot to a man."

She peered up at her daughter. "Are you angry at him?"

"Yes, but what's the point."

"You have no idea how angry I was at him back then. And it made me feel like a failure …"

There was a long pause while Nora struggled to search for the right words.

"So … if back then the gender choice had been possible, either I or Jillian would not be here."

Ennie looked her daughter straight in the eyes and took a while to speak.

"That's just about the size of it," she finally answered. "But," she hastened to add, "that doesn't mean he wasn't thrilled to have you and Jillian. It doesn't mean you or Jillian disappointed him. Never."

"I know," Nora said. "He never says it, but I've always known he loves us."

She took another long sip of her syncaf, deep in her own thoughts. All around them were the quiet voices of people sitting at the tables under the fruit trees. Servers climbed ladders, picked an apple or a pear, and put them on the customers' plate.

"And you, Mom?" Nora asked after a moment. "Did you ever want a boy?"

Ennie made a gesture of annoyance.

"Whatever it was that I wanted, I wanted it only because it would have made your father happy. Dear heavens," she blurted out. "What on earth does it matter if it's a girl or a boy?"

"Michael says it matters … Michael says we now have the choice, and the choice is a blessing."

Ennie put her hand on her daughter's.

"Michael is a good man. He has nothing but the best intentions. Does he put pressure on you? Because in that case —"

"Not pressure, but you know how he can be …"

"Yes, I know how he can be. Lead-footed sometimes."

Nora's voice cracked. "What if it happens to me too? What if we have a first-born daughter and I can't have any more children after her?"

"You know, Nora," Ennie said impatiently. "The only thing that bothers me about this business of the Parenting License is that it tries to cross every bridge before anybody gets there. All this planning, everyone trying to cover their behinds from the very beginning … I can't remember who said that progress means swapping one set of problems for another."

"But it's good that we talk about all these things, isn't it?"

"With or without the observers observing," Ennie reassured her.

"Dad says we should get potluck."

"That's what I say too. See if you can talk Michael into leaving the gender up to Mother Nature."

Nora grinned. "I wonder if *she* had to get a license before she could become a mother."

Ennie paid the bill and left a few keanus under the saucer.

"Probably not. She's been messing up since day one."

*　　*　　*

"We're going with potluck," Michael said.

Dr. Patel didn't reach for his pen just yet.

"And Nora is in full accord?"

"Yes," Michael replied, with as much conviction as he could put in his voice.

Dr. Patel searched in Michael's holochart for the item marked "Gender Preference," bypassed the 'F' and the 'M' and put a checkmark at 'N' for Natural.

"It must feel good to have left that problem behind," he said then.

"It does," Michael answered. "I was thinking … But it sounds pretentious."

"No, no, please finish your thought."

"I was thinking the DVP could split the parenting classes in two … For those applicant parents who make their own choice, that is."

"I'm not sure I follow."

"Well, you know … teach classes in parenting a boy and classes in parenting a girl."

Dr. Patel smiled. "Do you mind if I pass your idea to Mrs. Yamasaki? The DVP is always looking for suggestions. I imagine so far the thought was that it would be sexist to divide the genders."

"I'm surprised nobody thought of it," Michael said.

"I'm surprised myself," Dr. Patel agreed. "We have special courses for biracial parents, and you could very well argue that males and females are different races."

Nora laughed. It was the first time Dr. Patel had said something she found witty.

"I'm very happy to know that you have come to an agreement on the gender," Dr. Patel went on. "Now we can move on to other topics."

"Not the choice of writing implements again, I hope," Michael joked. "I'm not sure I did the right thing when I picked the silver fountain pen. It must have made me seem like quite the self-important male."

Dr. Patel shook his head. "There's no right or wrong," he corrected genially. "Just a personal choice."

"I would have thought my father-in-law would pick the silver fountain pen. Then again, Major Savins would have picked a stick if it had the logo of the Republic's Army on it," he added, but not sarcastically.

Dr. Patel remained politely noncommittal.

"How … how are we doing?" Michael asked then, ill at ease.

"You mean the therapy?"

"Yes."

"Well, we are making progress, and that is what matters."

"Yes," Michael said, "we are making progress."

The pun went unnoticed by Dr. Patel, busy at checking his schedule for the next available appointment.

"Tuesday the twentieth?"

"Tuesday the twentieth." Michael said. "Coming along in the marathon," he quipped.

The day the DVP men came to swap the babies with toddlers that could crawl, Nora decided it was time to start moving the furniture into the nursery.

It was sturdy furniture, all built with the latest safety features, and not too utilitarian as to be entirely ugly. Ennie was knitting blankets and baby clothes and Michael spent much of his free time putting in light fixtures, assembling the crib, and installing the room monitor. Even Nick popped by once in a while to help out, though mostly he ended up giving the wrong advice and getting on Michael's nerves.

There was a roundtable about what kind of wallpaper to choose. Again, the undetermined gender of the child made things a bit harder. It would have to be an all-purpose wallpaper.

"Not dinosaurs, I hope," Ennie said. "I never figured out why people love baby items with some nasty prehistoric beasts that ended up fossil fuel."

"The wallpaper with the blue sky and white clouds was nice," Nora proposed.

Michael nodded. "Yes, I like it too. I'll make a run to the store this afternoon."

The question of the name also came up more than once. Nora had said she wanted "Eva" for a girl, and she had said it in a way that didn't invite other suggestions.

"As long as Eva doesn't name *her* children Cain or Abel," Ennie joked. "In any case, it wouldn't be us teaching that old story."

Uncharacteristically, Nick had no objections to the rule forbidding religious indoctrination of minor children.

"If it can keep my grandkids from the terror of spending eternity in a lake of fire, absolutely," he conceded. "That's not religion, that's child abuse, if you ask me. We don't tell our children what profession to choose, or what party to vote for.

Why should we tell them what religion to follow? And while they're not even at the age of consent? Absurd."

"There's freedom of religion," he added, "and there's freedom *from* religion. Nobody dying in the name of some deity or other, and nobody killing in the name of some deity or other."

"All that 'My God is better than your God' nonsense," Ennie echoed.

"You don't suppose some parents give religious indoctrination on the sly?" Michael asked.

"Probably more than we can imagine," Nick answered.

"You know," Nick said then, getting more excited as he spoke, "Ennie and I voted for the secession because we thought the Parenthood Laws made a heap of sense. Jillian and Nora were little girls then, and we wanted to give them the best possible future. But now, here we all are, dealing for the first time with the actual business of the Laws. The more I see of the actual business of the Laws, the more I'm convinced that what looked good on paper is turning into a disaster."

"Remember communism?" Nick went on. "It was supposed to be paradise on earth. A lot of people all over the world fell for the idea — intelligent, compassionate people who had nothing but lovingkindness for humanity at large ... and look what a nightmare it became, the bastard child of good intentions."

"You wouldn't tell that to Doctor Patel, I hope?" Ennie joked to defuse the topic.

"Doctor Patel is the very picture of the well-intentioned idiot," Nick shot back. "But don't worry, he'll never know it from me."

While they were talking, Donny had crawled away from the blanket spread on the floor and, with his chubby hand, was stuffing a tuft of green yarn into his mouth. Ennie scooped him up and looked for Davy. Davy was under the desk, inspecting a paper clip with one end bent open.

"No, bad," Ennie said, her finger wagging.

She took away the tuft of yarn and the open paper clip, then burst into a laugh. "I don't suppose they understand me, do they?"

"Damn things," Nick grumbled.

Nora was napping on the living room sofa — or at least trying to. That day, she wanted nothing to do with babies, robotic or real. It was the August stretch at school, and she had a thick pile of tablets crammed with final exams to grade. The past few weeks, she'd withdrawn from everybody around her, in a state of misery she'd never known before.

There had been times lately when she couldn't help wondering whether she really wanted that baby that was sucking up her time and attention even before it was born.

Even with all the promises of help from family and friends, she knew that she was going to be the one who would miss peace of mind more than everybody else. She wanted to continue teaching, at least until the child would be in preschool. But even after preschool, every hour of her life would revolve around this creature she had decided to bring into the world without its consent.

Michael changed diapers and mixed formula, which she knew was more than a lot of new fathers did; but the truth was that she didn't want his help with the twins, just as she'd never wanted it with the housework. By the time she straightened out his mistakes, she could have done everything herself. She knew she wasn't the first woman who felt like that.

She would have to love this child very much, she thought. What a strange word "sacrifice" was — to make sacred, the dictionary said, "*to offer up something valuable.*" It was only now that she was coming to see how valuable was the life she had before she'd stepped into the Application Office. There must be something wrong with her, she worried, if she was so unwilling to make those sacrifices.

Worst of all, she didn't trust anybody with her secret worries, and she didn't need any observer to tell her that it was a capital mistake. Her hours with Dr. Patel were now filled with long pauses of painful silence. A few times she'd started to weep, only to worry even more when he didn't say a word, but looked at her with that gaze that seemed to miss nothing.

She'd begun to slip, and she knew it. In the parenting classes, Michael was the one who spoke up most of the time now, while she sat listlessly next to him thinking about something else. Michael never napped on the sofa away from the others, Michael never complained when the twins took away yet another hour of his sleep. He simply pulled her along with his unflagging desire to do everything right.

She now found his eagerness not endearing, but tiresome. She mustn't start to see him as an obstacle, she thought. They were in this together, weren't they? So many others had gone through this. Surely, she, too, could follow the rules, chalk up the steps. Then why was there a gaping fear inside her that she would never make it, not her?

*   *   *

But it was bound to happen, and she knew it.

During another joint session in which Michael alone had spoken for most of the hour, she started to weep into her hands and would not say a word more. Dr. Patel offered to move the next session to the following week, instead of two weeks, but that only seemed to drive Nora over the edge.

"No," she said harshly. "Nothing new will happen between now and a week, two weeks, or all the time in the world."

Michael looked at her, startled. Nora kept weeping quietly. She was lost in her own pain, and he didn't know how to break through. When he put his hand on hers, she pulled it away.

Dr. Patel bent his head toward her with a look of concern.

"We still have some time today," he offered. "Would you like to talk about what's making you so unhappy?"

Nora wadded her tissue and looked away from both men.

"Nightmares," she finally let out.

"Sweetie, tell me," Michael whispered. "Tell us," he corrected himself, making a gesture to include Dr. Patel.

Nora seemed to be fighting for air.

"Those mothers ..." she halted. "The ones who drown their babies ... drown them and bury them in their own blankets ..."

Her tears came back, muffled by her hands.

"You mean mothers with postpartum depression?" Dr. Patel asked.

"Yes," Nora sobbed. "What if I end up like them? You're not going to tell me you can diagnose that kind of psychosis before it happens?"

"No, unfortunately we still can't. But if you know the symptoms, you can spot them the moment they appear. And there is medication to treat postpartum depression."

Michael put his arm around Nora. "See? You're worried for nothing, sweetie."

Nora's head snapped as if he'd said something insulting.

"I worry for nothing? Who else should worry, Michael? It's not going to be you who gives birth and goes crazy ... Every risk here is on *my* plate. Whoever said women aren't the weaker sex didn't know what she was talking about!"

Michael didn't want to provoke her further, and remained silent. Dr. Patel, too, suppressed something he wanted to say.

Nora looked at the doctor. "And if I worry too much about everything that could or could not happen," she added hotly, "it's you people who got me into thinking that way. This whole 'marathon' is nothing but disaster preparedness, only there's a lot more to it than boarding up windows."

Again, the two men didn't try to contradict her.

Finally, Nora dabbed her eyes dry and tried to compose herself.

"I have nothing else to say. When someone can assure me that I will never kill my own children, I'll come back to sessions. Goodbye, Doctor." She got up and opened the door to step out.

Thinking she was out of earshot, Michael whispered, "It's okay, Doctor, we'll take the early appointment."

From the other side of the door Nora's voice was hoarse.

"Don't speak for me, Michael. I have a mind of my own."

Michael shook his head quietly to himself, then followed her.

*   *   *

"Nora honey, he's been crying for almost five minutes straight," Michael said at his wits' end.

Nora switched on another student's tablet and picked up her stylus.

"Let him cry. My father's right, they're just goddamn machines."

Michael was cradling Davy against his side, trying to soothe him as best he knew. Apparently, the parenting instructors didn't know how to do that anymore than he did; some things nobody knew.

"I'm really stumped here, honey. You take a look. Please," he begged.

Nora kept marking her students' tablets with her stylus, her back turned.

"I've got papers to grade. Let him cry."

Michael sighed loudly to himself. For a moment, he was tempted to put the squalling baby down and let him crawl in whatever disastrous direction he wanted.

"Let's call a sitter. Let's get out of the house. We're still in time to grab some dinner out," he said.

"I have to finish what I'm doing," Nora snarled. "You go grab some dinner out."

The noise had become unbearable. Michael tried the pacifier, then the juice bottle; nothing worked. It was a miracle that Donny, asleep in the temporary nursery with the door closed, couldn't hear his brother. For all Michael knew, what Davy wanted so desperately was precisely to wake up his brother.

"I'm not going out by myself," he countered.

"Then see what's in the fridge and let me do my work."

Michael lost his patience.

"You think you're the only one who has work to finish? I have to give a presentation tomorrow. I could use some peace and quiet too, you know."

Nora pushed aside her stylus.

"Fine. Fifty-fifty then, like always."

She got up, grabbed hold of the baby's arm and yanked him up from Michael's lap with a single motion. Davy's head whipped back in mid-air, then forward again. His mouth went slack; his head flopped over against his chest and the body went limp. Now there was silence.

"Finally," Nora said.

She put the baby down in his playpen and went back to her tablets on the desk.

Michael got up with a speed she didn't register right away. Flat on his back, Davy lay perfectly still, his arms splayed open, his eyes lifted to the ceiling with a glassy stare. He picked him up with all the care Nora hadn't remembered to use. He looked hard at the small still face, patted the baby's cheek a few times, got no response.

"Oh God."

Again, Nora didn't notice what Michael was doing.

"Put him in his crib," she told him. "Now they'll sleep through the night."

Michael said, "Nora."

"What? What is it now?"

Michael picked up the limp baby and brought him over so she could see him.

"Nora, he's dead."

Once again Nora pushed aside her stylus and turned for a look.

"Yeah, right. Some sick sense of humor you have."

"I'm serious, Nora." He lay the baby down on the desk.

"Watch the tablets," Nora said.

Davy wasn't moving. Not a twitch, not a hiccup. His eyes were like ponds that had frozen over.

"Nora, he's dead," Michael said again.

This time Nora gave the baby her full attention.

She'd never seen a dead body, but what lay on top of her scattered tablets was a dead body. Shock made her as still as that baby that was no longer a baby, but a piece of destroyed machinery. Instinctively, she grabbed the baby by the shoulders and would have started to shake it, if Michael hadn't stopped her.

"You shook him enough," he said hoarsely.

He sat down across from her and, for a very long while, they stared at the small body dressed in his blue jammies with the yellow ducks. Nora put her hand across her mouth to keep herself from screaming. The next few minutes were filled with all the quiet they had wished for in all the past months.

"All I did was pick him up," she murmured. "Michael, I just picked him up."

"You picked him up the wrong way. Can't you remember *anything* from all those classes?"

"Ah … I did pick him up hard, didn't I?"

She listened intently in the direction of the nursery. Donny must be still asleep, but she had to check. Who knows what a twin did when one of the pair died.

She rushed into the nursery and looked into the crib in the dim nightlight. She felt the baby's head under her hand, put her finger under his nose and waited for the faint breath that moved in and out of his lungs. It was there. She felt a great surge of relief, just before she remembered that she had to go back to the baby that would never breathe again, to Michael who would never trust her again.

There was a dull buzzing in her ears, like the echo of all the crying she'd heard from the moment she'd gotten the babies. The thought flashed in her mind of the holofolder on Mrs. Yamasaki's desk. She saw the woman tossing the holofolder into the incinerator, and her heart sank. She started sobbing uncontrollably.

Her first instinct — like a little girl, she thought — was to call her mother. *And tell her what?* she wondered, with a wave of nausea. She sank into a chair away from the desk, away from what she had ruined.

How many times had she heard her mother remind her never to do what she'd just done? How many times had she heard just about everybody give the same warning? Didn't she know the damn machines were programmed to have their spine snapped precisely like a shaken baby?

Michael had picked up the dead body and put it back in the playpen. He was staring at it as if just by staring at it he could bring it back to life.

For the next ten minutes, they argued like they'd never argued in their lives, walking toward each other, and then away from each other, like combatants in a duel. "If only you had" and "If only you hadn't" came and went, fear and shock and anger flung back and forth between them.

Eventually Michael sat down. "There has to be a solution … We can try to get another baby from the DVP," and, even as he was saying that, he knew there was no way of getting another baby from the DVP. "We can tell them it was damaged, and pay the fine …"

"They check," Nora said between tears, again only stating the obvious. "They want the damaged baby back before they issue another."

Michael ran his hand over his hair, as if trying to shield himself from a falling object.

"Then who could help us?" he asked himself more than her. "Someone at school …"

"I don't trust anybody at school. You never know who could call the DVP on us."

Imagine Marina Tafwe getting wind of it, Nora thought, and now there was a rush of precisely that burning shame and guilt she'd tried to use on the rebellious seventeen-year-old.

"This isn't happening," Michael said. "This just isn't happening."

"Alan and Steve?" Nora ventured.

"What would they know that we don't? I'm sure they know how *not* to pick up their baby, though."

Nora started sobbing again. She'd never thought her own husband would be the first to turn against her.

From the nursery came Donny's wail, growing louder under their raised voices. There was another baby who was alive and well and demanding the same attention as ever.

Michael went to pick him up, and was about to put him in the playpen, when he remembered that Donny's twin lay lifeless in it. He removed the dead baby, hid it behind the drapes, then lowered Donny into the playpen, among the stuffed toys his brother had played with until half an hour before.

"This just can't be happening," he said again under his breath.

"Isn't there some sort of underground market for the machines?" Nora said, and she couldn't believe she was asking that question. *An applicant mother looking for babies in the underground market,* she thought.

Michael absently put a bottle of juice in the playpen and let Donny feed himself.

"Even if there was, what would it change?" he said. "You still killed him."

Nora didn't reply. The weight of what she had done was beginning to sink in. It was the worst thing she'd ever felt.

"Nothing," Michael said then, "we'll just have to tell everybody what happened, then we'll just have to wait these last three months until the year is over and —"

"Turn in the second application," Nora finished.

What else was there to do?

SIX

MICHAEL DIDN'T FORGIVE HER RIGHT AWAY, but he forgave her. It was Nora who didn't forgive herself. A stubborn sadness came down on her, tinged everything she did. Dr. Patel would have told her it was anger directed at herself, but she knew better. The ones she was really angry at were all those anonymous strangers who had saddled her with all those rational choices she had balked at from the start.

Either those strangers were wrong, or she was, but she had reached the point where she no longer cared about sorting out her confusion. From now on, she decided, she would make her own misguided choices, and learn to live with them if she could. For Mrs. Nora Holmes Savins, the marathon was over.

Michael went alone to the Department of Vital Privileges, filled in the request of withdrawal, and in the box, "Reason for withdrawal", put the truth of what had happened: "Death of child due to shaken-baby syndrome."

He considered it a minor stroke of luck that he didn't have to face Mrs. Yamasaki in person this time. But he would have to face her again in three months, and the thought filled him with dread.

Then he went through the long sequence of calling each observer, and explaining to each observer, the truth of what had happened. The worst part was having to listen to the veiled reproach he could hear between the lines of what were, for all intents and purposes, their condolences. You have wasted our time, each one of those observers seemed to be saying — our time and yours.

Finally, he called the various agencies that had supplied the babies, and the returnable baby supplies, and he had them come pick everything up. The entire time the movers were going in and out of what had been her temporary nursery, Nora hid in the bathroom sobbing.

She insisted on paying the fine for the damaged HumaNew: four months' worth of her salary. Somewhere in a factory in North Korea, Davy and Donny Holmes would get a new life as someone else's children. Their features that were a blend of Michael's and Nora's would be erased and reprogrammed; whenever she thought of that, it was almost like mourning a real death.

Her parents were shocked, but not at her. Nick was especially angry.

"If it had been a real baby, even someone else's baby, you would have never been careless," Nick said. "Do these idiots at the DVP really think you would handle a goddamn piece of machinery as you would a child? Let's tell them that," he said vehemently. "Let's raise a holy stink with these people. There must be a lot of others who went through the same thing. Let's put our heads together, we and whoever else has to deal with this garbage."

"And you suppose that when it's time for the second application, the DVP will forget that we raised a holy stink?" Ennie countered.

"Let's just start again three months from now," Michael said, "and then we'll see." He looked at Nora. "I'm sure you won't kill *two* babies." He wanted to sound facetious, but Nora winced.

Nora had stayed out of the conversation. Ennie had already told her that she was worried about her, and the thing that worried her the most was that Nora refused to talk about the matter with anybody.

Then there were the explanations that needed to be given to friends and coworkers, to all those who'd toasted them at their wedding and wished them a wait no longer than three hundred and sixty-five days.

At school, Nora came up with an excuse that she was sure everybody would see through. The therapists, she said, had found serious fault lines between the generations that needed to be healed before the child came. It didn't make her or anybody in her family look good, but anything was better than having to reveal the real reason why she'd been deferred.

What an example she would make for her young students if they knew the truth, she thought. Her entire existence had come crashing down, and all for a moment of carelessness, an instant of frustration. The times she felt worst, of course, was when she thought she could have killed a real child, her own or someone else's.

Michael didn't believe in crying over spilled milk, and he wasn't easily defeated. But Nora now found that infuriating instead of comforting. At the start of the new year, the moment the Department of Vital Privileges reopened after Founding Father's Day, Michael walked into Mrs. Yamasaki's office and handed her another holofolder, marked "Reproduction – Application Two."

Nora waited outside. If Mrs. Yamasaki wanted to talk to her, she thought, Mrs. Yamasaki would have to come out and talk to her. She wondered whether there was a review board where she would have to defend her actions and petition to be given a second chance, like a convict seeking parole.

But Michael emerged from the office with an encouraging grin.

"All set," he said. "Not a word from our Mrs. Yamasaki. I just handed her the folder, she put it on the pile to her right and sent me on my way. Thank goodness she kept me out of her family parade this time."

Nora made no comment.

"I need to stop by the pharmacy to pick up my birth control pills," she said then.

"But I've been taking *my* pills."

"No. I want to go back to mine," she insisted.

She seemed to be searching for the right words, and she added quickly, "I need to learn responsibility."

Michael started the car and didn't argue with her. He reminded himself that she was the same woman with whom he'd come to bring the first application, so many long months ago. But she didn't smile or laugh as much as she used to.

He chalked everything up to the trauma of her having failed the application, and didn't press for explanations. During their joint therapy with the new psychologist, Nora spoke in monosyllables most of the time, and revealed nothing except generic facts that Michael or her family could confirm.

All of their psychologists had been changed, as per the DVP's rule. Of course, Nora thought, their previous cadre of psychological pest control might have overlooked some termites in the basement.

Their medical doctors had been kept on, and Dr. Canetti was still their general practitioner. It was a good thing, because Dr. Canetti was the most compassionate of their observers, and never chided Nora or anybody else for the death of the baby.

"It happens," Dr. Canetti said simply. "It's only a machine, right?"

"But it changes you," Nora said. "Machine or not."

Michael was startled. It was the first time since the loss of the application that Nora was saying something even remotely personal. It seemed strange that she had let out that confession in the presence of their medical doctor and not of their psychologist.

"Well, as far as your health is concerned, the two of you are at the peak of your reproductive years," Dr. Canetti reassured them. "One more year won't make much difference."

"Good to know," Michael said, and it was indeed the best piece of news he'd heard in a while.

Dr. Canetti addressed Nora. "You mentioned you're the one taking birth control now?"

"Yes," Nora said. "I figured I'd give Michael a break." She tried a grin. "The pill makes him moody."

Dr. Canetti chuckled. "Let me make a note of the change. Now, as far as our next appointment is concerned, I won't need to see you again for three months. You started attending your classes again?"

"This time we're just breezing through," Michel replied. "More often than not, we spend our free time as a second honeymoon."

Dr. Canetti nodded, smiling. "Most deferred patients do. The DVP has no problem with it. We need our applicant parents to be in good emotional shape."

She checked her tablet again. "So, I have you down for the last week of January. Is that okay?"

"That's fine," Michael said.

He had a surprise planned for Nora for the rest of the day: a visit to the terraforming exhibit that had just opened downtown. Nora followed him without objections, doing her best to seem interested in the life cycle of Martian xenospores.

Waiting for them at home was their new baby. This time the DVP had shipped a girl. She was born in perfect health, and she made only the minimum of fuss. But Nora refused to leave her with a sitter, and had taken to giving unwanted advice to those members of her family with whom she did leave the baby.

She treated the newborn as if she were made of crystal, but everybody could see how much she hated that thing. She'd stayed out of the naming, rejecting everyone's suggestions without offering any of her own, until Ennie had proposed, "Why not Eva, since we all like that?"

Nora turned on her mother with uncharacteristic harshness.

"No. Eva is for my *real* daughter. Pick anything else for the microchip."

And "the microchip" it had remained for her, or "the baby" when she felt a little less bitter.

Michael had stopped taking his contraceptives now that Nora had insisted on being the one in charge. Nora kept her pills in their pink round box on the bathroom vanity; had Michael been so inclined, he could have kept track of each day and each pill. But he was too relieved at his freedom from his contraceptive routine to bother with making sure Nora followed hers.

It was true that second children raised themselves, Nora thought. Even the sound of the baby's crying was less alarming, and, with no twin to attend to, two arms at a time were enough. The baby girl was patient enough to wait until her formula was ready, instead of squalling for it. She seemed to have been endowed with the ability to soothe herself rather than impose her demands on those around her.

Her features again were a blend of Michael's and Nora's, in fact more pronounced, as if the DVP were trying to make it easier for the parents to love this baby more, so that this baby would be better treated than the first. The DVP even offered support groups for bereaved parents, which Nora thought was the height of inanity.

Meanwhile, Alan and Steve had been granted their License on their first application, and now their certified surrogate mother was two-months pregnant with their first child. They had chosen a boy. The CSM had been inseminated at the same time with sperm from both men, so that either Alan or Steve could be the father.

When the pregnancy was confirmed, they had thrown a lavish party, but Michael had had to argue with Nora to make her attend. He told her he understood why she didn't want to go, but it had to be done.

After Nora finally agreed, she spent a morning alone shopping for a present. She'd come home with a gift boxed in a variation of the most popular wrap, the one with angel babies holding in their hands a scrolled Parenting License. The cartoon over their heads read: "Thank you, Daddy and Daddy!" She thought it would be a waste of money to personalize the wrap with the names of the daddies.

For her present, she had decided to splurge on a pair of used denim overalls. After the cotton crash, denim had become too expensive to produce, and all that could be found were pricey items on the vintage market. Nora had liked the overalls so much she'd bought another pair to keep.

"This one is for *our* baby," she'd explained cheerfully. "Too cute to let them slip."

It was the first thing she'd bought with an eye to the future, and Michael thought it was a very good sign that she was healing. Nora put the overalls in a drawer in their bedroom, not with the things loaned by the DVP. As time went by, Michael forgot all about them. It wasn't until months later that he noticed they were gone. By then, Nora was gone too.

SEVEN

IT WAS THE ONLY BABY THING SHE COULD TAKE WITH HER, those denim overalls. All those baby things donated by all those anonymous strangers were marked with the strangers' logo, and would give her away in an instant.

What an exhausting time it had been since she had made up her mind. Months of covering her tracks like a criminal, because a criminal was what she had become.

Secretly driving to a pawnshop to sell every piece of jewelry she owned, except those given to her by her husband; driving to a different pawnshop to sell the most expensive of her wedding presents, and then telling her parents she had lost it; taking from her bank account one bit at a time all the money she owned; searching the house for the last place where her husband would look for the cash; buying new luggage that was easier to carry. Months of secretly preparing for war.

Someone else she had deceived was the female student from whom she had obtained the negative sample in exchange for an undeserved college-entrance grade.

She had told the student she needed the sample because of a trespass with a recreational drug, and the student had been canny enough to pretend that her teacher was telling the truth. Of course, the student could have been pregnant and given her a useless sample; and of course, the student might tell on her. Her secret war demanded cunning and gambles she had never anticipated in her life.

Yet another person she had deceived was her physician, paid by the nation to find out how its citizens reproduced. She did not know whether physicians were paid also to denounce citizens who reproduced against the laws of the nation. She wondered whether the Founding Fathers and Founding Mothers had ever imagined that, in their world born of good intentions, nobody would be able to trust anybody.

The longest of those long days before her flight were those she spent waiting for the physician to call her. When the call finally came, and all was lawful in the eyes of the nation, the last thread was cut, and she was on her way.

While her husband was at work, she took the denim overalls out of the bedroom drawer and wrapped them tightly inside one of her sweaters. First, she held the overalls for a moment against her face, as if smelling already the baby that would wear them in their new country — if they ever reached their new country. She closed her new easy-to-carry suitcase, put it in the trunk of her car, sat at the wheel, and started to drive without a look back at her house.

Perhaps it was better to give up, she had thought more than once, when her eyes started to blur and her hands to shake on the wheel. What good was it to persist in her defiance — life was more important, was it not, a higher good than freedom? There were times when she was not sure she wanted to be free at such a cost. She was alone now. Nothing to stay with her except that other heartbeat echoing just under her own, that other life that got sick if she got sick, died if she died, and — so the experts said — got sad if she got sad.

She made the crossing at two in the afternoon, in broad daylight, as if she had nothing to hide, wearing a light parka to disguise her belly that was beginning to show. The Pregnancy Police and the bounty hunters were trained to spot the signs: cracker crumbs from a bout of morning sickness, the indentation of a stretched maternity panel visible under too sheer a blouse.

She was visiting a relative, was the answer she had ready, along with the name and telephone number of a cousin they could have called to check. If they did call to check, they would start hunting her down the minute the cousin told them he wasn't expecting her; but it was a better cover than nothing. She watched the guards check her passport, and remembered that the last time she had used her passport was on her honeymoon. But she must not think about that.

She would not have been the first woman being hunted down. Husbands wanted their children, and grandparents their grandchildren; the entire nation wanted its children. The country on the other side of the border did not send the runaways back. In fact, she had heard rumors of something called an underground railway, the name invented for those who helped runaway slaves long ago. But she had never considered looking for helpers. She trusted no one anymore.

She counted it a stroke of good luck that, when she had turned eighteen, she had chosen to remove the tiny transceiver microchip that her parents had had implanted in her forearm the day she was born, as most parents did. Thanks also to her decision to have the chip removed, she had made it across, even bantering a few phrases with the border guards, while each minute ticked away.

Where had she found the courage, she wondered, the easy demeanor that would not set the guards off? When she was a girl, her parents had always been peeved at her shyness, at how she would rather walk with a swollen toe than tell anyone her shoe pinched.

Perhaps it had not been shyness, she thought with a secret smile. Perhaps it had been the same silent, stubborn strength that had seen her now into a new country, a world away from everything she had ever known.

If she ever went back, the thing she would remember most about the new country was the cold. It dragged on the blood inside her veins; it stopped her feet from moving, and her lips from making a sound. It made the world a place of shivery blue. At times, it seemed there was no place where she could escape it, where she could keep warm the child inside her. And this child inside her, this new life that her old country had damned even before it was born, would it ever know anything but the cold?

The child was still nameless. Boy, girl … who knew? That too was defiance. Back where she was running away from, by now she would have known every single thing that could be known about this new life, down to whether the hair would be curly or straight, the disposition sunny or melancholic.

Back where she was running away from were her husband, her father, her mother, her sister, her friends, and the white and blue clouds on the wallpaper of the empty nursery. Would her child ever see any of them and any of that? she wondered. What was she going to tell her child when her child would ask why she had denied all that was its birthright?

She was six months along now, and feeling every discomfort of her condition. It had become hard to stand for more than a few hours in the bookstore where she had found the job that fed her and her hungry new life. It had become hard to sleep, with the baby kicking restlessly in the night. But what an amazing thing it was, the feel of that tiny hard skull just under her skin, just to the right of her belly button.

At some other time, her small studio apartment must have housed a college student who had no plans of becoming a parent anytime soon. She did not know where she would put the baby's things, but she would find a place; her baby would have so many fewer things anyway.

The first thing she had bought was the crib: white with dancing teddy bears. She had picked one with the rocking springs and the heartbeat machine. Sometimes, she turned the heartbeat machine on, to hear it echo softly next to her when she lay in her twin bed.

Funny, she thought, that they should call it a twin bed when it was made for one person. And funny that, when she thought about twins, she remembered some dolls she had once treated as she would have treated flesh and blood. At times, she could not help thinking that she would have welcomed even their company now.

A roll of second-hand baby clothes was stored in the second-hand bathing tub. The changing table she could do without, and a friend from the bookstore would let her have the stroller her child did not need anymore. She remembered her Irish grandmother, who had never bought a newborn's crib; instead, she would pull a bottom drawer out of a dresser and line it well with blankets. Her grandmother used to say that her babies had a crib in every house.

Out of loneliness, she had made herself take the first steps with the women she had met in the physician's office. Expectant mothers formed a society of their own, as new to her as this country itself. Neither the physician nor the women ever asked her where the baby's father was, or why she had run away. No one in the new country thought that some children were children of the wrong time.

Out of need, she did not refuse when some of the women invited her over for a meal. But it was hard for her to sit alone among their children and husbands, parents and siblings, the circle of loving people she had left behind.

She did not refuse when the women gave her maternity clothes and baby things they no longer needed. No showers from designated enforcers in this country. No largesse that became property on a date set by strangers, providence with endless strings attached. Here she had come to rely on the sympathy of new friends who understood why she had left her circle of loving people behind, friends who admired her for having gained her freedom without anybody's help.

She spent Saturday afternoons in thrift shops, blaming herself for never having learned from her mother how to knit or sew. Perhaps now she could have saved on blankets and new clothes, and while away the empty time in the evenings when there was no other sound in the house except that of her own feet coming and going.

When she let in the thought of her mother, of her father and sister, of her husband, she blamed herself for the despair that must surely be flowing into her child with the very cells of her blood.

As for the child, nothing was known except that it existed. She did not want to know anything else, not until the child took its first breath. Her old country would have thought it supreme selfishness to burden with all these unknowns a creature that had not asked to be created, when it was so easy to map so many of the unknowns, and to erase the ones that meant a difficult life.

The old nightmares had never left her. Babies born without faces, without limbs; babies born with perfect faces and perfect

86

limbs who, some years down the line, developed diseases and defects no one could name.

Was she ready, she wondered, for something that would have meant a difficult life? No one here would make her sign a clause for a disease or defect; no one would suggest that she rid herself of a difficult life before it was born. This was her responsibility alone. Everything was on her shoulders, and everything was on her head.

She had told the physician she did not want to see the pictures every other woman in his waiting room was so impatient to see — the pictures they called the first portrait of their child. *Potluck,* her father said, as it had been for millions of years before the physicians grew to know so much. So, she had decided, if some things had to be left to luck, then all things would be left to luck. How else would she learn the hard lessons, the ones she had forgotten the first time?

She missed her husband with a pain that seemed to choke her in the night, when she turned in the bed and no one was beside her. How he would have liked to feel her body taut with the baby. She was still in time, she thought, when the despair grew too strong. He would come to her; he would forgive her, she thought. What good man doesn't want to see what he has made.

But perhaps her husband was no longer the same good man who trusted her. Perhaps he was now just another bounty hunter who would tear her child away from her without a moment's hesitation. Her family, too … Who knows whether they may have turned against her. She had upended the expected legacy of all of them, changed all their future.

Only a few more weeks left now, the toughest ones. The white crib with the dancing teddy bears stood waiting by her bed.

*   *   *

It was a girl. It was her Eva — for whom she had traded everything. Eva had ten fingers and ten toes and everything where it should be for the time being; but there were no guarantees, on the big things or on the small ones.

This one was flesh and blood. This one was hers and her husband's, created by them and carrying the genes of all the generations before them. This one was their daughter and, if some of those genes harbored the worst of secrets, only time and hard patience would tell. Eva was plump and long like a small sleek animal, and suckled with all the force of life in her. Her father would have loved her, born at the wrong time or not.

He and her family must be searching everywhere for her. Imagining them going door to door filled her with anguish. She remembered her husband's dear and earnest desire to do everything as it must be done, who was now doing what he had never wanted to do.

There was no going back. There was this new life that must be accounted for, a life that had the right to the best possible start in spite of a destiny that she had shifted somewhere else even before she had conceived it.

She watched the news from her old country obsessively: a runaway in her seventh month pushed by her angry parents toward the van where the Pregnancy Police was waiting, a young man on trial for marrying a woman in her forties who wanted a husband on paper so she could have a child who had been denied to her too many times.

How had it come to this? she marveled. How had everybody been led to believe with all their hearts that this was for the good of the country? And how had she herself been led to believe that, until she had found what was either the courage or the foolishness not to believe it anymore? The only thing that kept her going was the cry of her daughter in the night, before her daughter fell asleep, still safe from knowing what her mother knew.

*   *   *

At last, one day, Nora, who had once been Nora Holmes Savins, bought a pretty postcard of her cold new country and mailed it to her husband with a postmark as plain as day, like a line thrown across a pond that someone may or may not catch.

"She is three months old and she looks like you," the postcard said. "Come stay with us."

Some time later — she lost track of the time, because the time was terrifying — there was a knock at her door. Her heart leapt to her throat. These days, every time there was a knock at her door, her heart leapt to her throat. She wanted to stand up, but could not move. Was it her husband, and had he come to welcome them back? Was it a bounty hunter, and had he come to force them back?

Either welcoming or forcing — back to what? Punishment accepted, because nothing else was possible? Eva growing up in the old country, all her years spent under the weight of her mother's guilt and shame? Every warning, every lesson that had been hammered into her came back in a pained jumble. Loved by the right people in the right way for the right reasons and at the right time. Could any of that still be true for her own flesh and blood?

This could not go on. She would not spend her life in fear, with endless questions gnawing at her soul.

The knock came again. She stood up, kissed Eva's forehead, and went to open the door.

YOU MIGHT ALSO ENJOY

THE IRON AND THE LOOM
A Novel of Italy

by Flavia Idà

How many times, she wondered, had she woven together cloth that his sword had then torn apart along with the flesh underneath?

The Last Speck of the World

by Flavia Idà

No name. No race. No nationality. The survivor of the perfect catastrophe struggles to preserve herself and her hope that she may be found — by humans.

THE NAMES OF HEAVEN

by Flavia Idà

One man. An extraordinary choice.

Available from Paper Angel Press in
hardcover, trade paperback, and ebook editions.
paperangelpress.com

www.ingramcontent.com/pod-product-compliance
Lightning Source LLC
Chambersburg PA
CBHW020633130626
46552CB00003B/1206